Nick S. Klaus

The Snowberry Series Book 7

Katie Mettner

Copyright © 2015 Katie Mettner

All rights reserved

The characters and events portrayed in this book are fictitious. Any similarity to real persons, living or dead, is coincidental and not intended by the author.

No part of this book may be reproduced, or stored in a retrieval system, or transmitted in any form or by any means, electronic, mechanical, photocopying, recording, or otherwise, without express written permission of the publisher.

ISBN-10 : 1517221048
ISBN-13 : 978-1517221041

Cover design by: Carrie Butler
Printed in the United States of America

*Believe in the spirit of the season and
the magic of love, forever.*

Chapter One

I leaned against the doorjamb and quietly contemplated the woman at the piano. She had her back turned to me, but it didn't take a degree in elementary education to see she was crying. The sniffing and eye wiping were dead giveaways. Her right hand was playing one note repeatedly, as though she was stuck on what the next note of the song was. Since she's the music teacher at John Peter Thomas Elementary School, JPT for short, I didn't think that was the case. I think she was stuck on life. Of course, if you had the guts to say that to her, she would vehemently deny it, and probably punch you.

I raised my hand and knocked once. I didn't want to scare her by walking up behind her, but I did want to talk to her. "Mandy?" I asked, following the knock, and I saw her shoulders slump at the sound of my voice. Her obvious disdain for me was always such a boost to my self-esteem.

"I don't want to talk, Nick," she said softly, her fingers playing the second note of the song, and the third and the fourth. I recognized the tune. *Cry Me a River*. I smiled, since she couldn't see me, and sat on a chair behind her back. I let her play out the song and when the room was silent, I leaned forward on my elbows.

"Why are you crying a river?" I asked the beautiful, sad woman at the piano. The warm September afternoon had sweat trickling down my back. I hated being caged up in this little, windowless room, but I would sit here as long as I had to in order to find out why she was crying.

"I'm not."

I leaned back and crossed my feet at my ankles. "That's funny, because I've been standing at the door for the last five minutes witnessing your crying, or do you have allergies?"

She whipped around and pointed her finger at me. "Can't I get any privacy around here?"

I shook my head to the negative. "This is an elementary school. If you want privacy, you aren't going to find it here."

"School is out, and the kids are gone. I'm alone here. I should think that would afford me a little privacy, except, apparently, my nosy co-workers never learned the definition of it."

"While it's true the kids are gone, if you really want to cry unbothered by your nosy co-workers, you probably shouldn't do it sitting on your piano bench with the door open. Just sayin' …"

She stood up in a huff and slammed the cover down on the piano, stomping to the cubby near the wall for her purse. She tucked it under her arm, haughtily, and shut off the lights.

"I'm leaving, which means you are, too. At least my room. Feel free to slink through the halls and eavesdrop on other people."

I uncurled myself from the chair and sauntered over to her, my hands in my pockets. "It's only three-thirty, aren't you going to wait for your kids, Mands?" I asked, my brow arched towards the ceiling.

"My kids are with my ex for the weekend, and don't call me Mands!" She took off in a huff and slammed the door behind her hard enough to shake the walls.

I rocked back on my heels and eyed the door. It appeared Mandy Alexander had a bee in her bonnet. I would bet this week's salary it had everything to do with her ex, again.

"Scotch on the rocks, two rocks only," Wes recited, setting the familiar glass in front of me.

"Thanks, Wes." I smiled gratefully at the old man who owned Wes' Saloon. It was the oldest bar in Snowberry, Minnesota, but resembled a saloon about as much as an elephant resembles a cat.

He gave me a salute and meandered down the bar to help another customer. I took a drink of the scotch and it burned as it went down. The bar was busy and ridiculously loud, but it was Friday night. This was the only place to find food, drink, and dancing all in the same place. I glanced around the newly remodeled space to see several teachers from the district on the dance floor, and two more in a booth, sharing a plate of wings.

It appeared that everyone was celebrating a successful first week of school, except for one woman. I looked deep into the scotch to distract myself, but all I saw was Mandy Alexander's face reflected in the cubes of melting ice. I tossed the rest of the drink down my throat and slammed the glass onto the edge of the bar for a refill.

Something hit my left forearm and I turned to see a basket of popcorn resting next to it. A few of the kernels had spilled out of the bowl on its ride from the other end of the bar.

Wes motioned at them and said, "Clean up your mess."

"You're the one who made the mess," I shot back, grabbing one of the pieces of corn from the bar and throwing it at him. He put his hand on his hip and I started to snicker. He looked just like Squidward from SpongeBob when he did that.

"You've had three shots of whiskey in less than thirty minutes. If you don't eat something soon, you're going to fall off my barstool, and then we're both going to be in the paper."

I rolled my eyes and shoved a handful of popcorn in my mouth, chewing noisily for his benefit. He didn't move to refill my drink, so I leaned over the bar toward him. "Was it really three shots? I guess I lost count."

He took the rocks glass and set it under the bar, filling a mug with Diet Coke and sliding it to me. "That's because your mind is somewhere else. The bar could burn down and you wouldn't notice."

I swirled the straw in the glass to kill the foam. "The first week of school just ended. You know how tiring that is."

He leaned an elbow on the bar and moved his finger in and out of the crowd. "I see at least ten teachers in this establishment who don't look like their mother just died."

"Being a teacher and being a principal are two completely different things, Wes."

He grabbed a beer glass that came sailing down the bar and stuck it under the tap. "That's right, the teachers are the ones who actually work."

I laughed and pegged another piece of corn at him, which he dodged with no problem. He slid the beer back down the bar the way only a seasoned tender can.

"Were there problems this week, Nick? I've seen you every Friday night since you moved into this town five years ago. Your mug is ugly enough without that scowl you've been wearing all night."

I laughed sarcastically. "Funny. I'm not wearing a scowl." I glanced up into the bar mirror and saw the look he spoke of. I relaxed my brows and tried to make my face look cheerful.

"You look like you've either been sucking on lemons or something more than school is bothering you. Like, say, a woman."

I took another long pull on the Diet Coke. I could feel the scotch making my head fuzzy and knew I wouldn't be having anymore tonight. "I'm worried about one of my teachers. I don't know why. I'm going to go for a walk." I slid off the barstool and threw a twenty on the bar. "Have a great night, Wes."

Before he could answer, his cook came through the door with a take-out order. "Here's Mandy's order, boss. She said to call when it was ready and she would come down."

My foot hesitated on the next step and I turned back to the bar. "I'm heading home. I'll take it to her, Wes," I yelled over the din of the crowd.

I fought my way back to the bar and he raised a brow. "I'm not so sure Mandy wants you hand-delivering her meal, Nick. She sees enough of you during the week."

I leaned in over the bar and lowered my voice. "I found her crying at the piano before I left school today. The food gives me an excuse to check on her."

Wes' brow went nearly to the sky. "Mandy's got a family to check on her, Nick. She doesn't need her boss breathing down her throat."

I looked around. "Okay, where's her family, Wes?" I held up my hands to motion around the room and he frowned. "Besides, I'm not her boss tonight. I'm her next-door neighbor."

He relented and lowered his brow. At least he

no longer resembled Ernie from Sesame Street. "She hasn't paid for the food."

I opened my wallet and took out another twenty, tossing it on the bar, and picking up the white plastic container. "Keep the change."

He held up the money as I walked away. "If she comes looking for me, I'm gonna tell her you coerced me!"

I laughed and raised my hand in acknowledgment as I opened the door. I was never more thankful for the fresh night air on my face. The door closed to the loud bar and I sighed in relief on the quiet street. I had about five minutes to think about what I was going to say to Mandy when I was standing on her steps with her meal in my hand. I could always use the *I was heading home* excuse if worse came to worse.

Mandy Alexander has been my neighbor for five years. We did neighborly things, like wave at each other from the driveway, borrow a cup of sugar, and occasionally I play a little B-ball with her son, Ben, but that's where it ends. It wasn't me, it was her. She refused to share anything personal. She was always receptive and cooperative at school, but when it came to anything social, she had a gigantic, *not interested* sign flashing on her forehead.

I knew she didn't date, Ben made sure I was aware of his mother's single status, but so far, I haven't gotten a foot in the door. I looked down at the food in my hand. I must be crazy for doing this. Maybe the first week of school had fried all the common sense from my brain. It was too late to turn back now, though.

Wes' Saloon was two minutes from home if I walked slowly, so before I could finish thinking of a story to tell her, I was standing in front of her house. The lights were on inside the brick ranch home. I realized this would be the first time I saw the inside of her house in five years. That is if I made it past the front door.

I shook my head and laughed. Don't count on that happening, Nick. She'll probably take the food and slam the door in your face. I jogged up the steps two at a time and raised my hand to the door. I knocked twice and waited, but no one came. Had she left to get the food already? I jumped back down the steps and paused. I would have passed her on her way to Wes' if she went to pick it up. She had to be here somewhere.

I heard music and cocked my head, straining to hear what direction it might be coming from. Is that Celine Dion? I followed the path around the side of the house and stopped at the edge of the lawn. Mandy was in a floral pillow covered chaise lounge with her legs under a blanket and a fire going in the oil burning pit. She was hanging up the phone when I stepped around the corner.

"You better not have eaten my food, Nick Klaus," she growled.

I approached her carefully and handed her the container. "It's all there. How did you know I was here?"

She rolled her eyes toward the sky for a minute. "I'm a teacher and a mom. I have eyes in the back of my head. Besides, you were about as quiet as a bull in a china shop."

"And Wes just called to tell you I was on my way with your dinner, right?" I asked, plopping down into a matching lawn chair across from her. The garish red flowers had faded in the summer sun to an ugly rust brown. It reminded me of an old set my parents used to have from the 70s.

She flipped open the container and popped a fry in her mouth. "He may have mentioned something about not wanting bloodshed when you arrived. He's so immature."

I tried not to laugh at her. She was amusing when she wasn't being Queen B of the Universe. I really don't know why I find her so interesting and alluring when she clearly isn't interested in dating anyone. Maybe it's because I know it's an act. She's wonderful with the kids at school, and I've seen her with her own kids. She's a very loving woman, but she has a big problem with men. And that's a bigger problem for me since I am one.

"Do you make it a habit of staring at women while they eat?" she asked, laying the burger back in the container.

"Sorry, I was just thinking about what a lovely space you have back here."

"Lovely? Are you a sixty-year-old woman?"

She took another bite of her burger and I

leaned toward her, clasping my hands together. "You know, Mands, what's with the constant snark? I was just complimenting your backyard. I wasn't trying to get in your pants."

"But you wouldn't mind if you did, right?" she asked around the fry in her mouth.

I stood up and shook my head at her. "My, you do think highly of yourself. Have a good night, Mandy."

I turned and stalked across the yard and through the hedge of trees, coming out on my driveway. I could hear her calling to me as I unlocked my back door, so I made sure to slam it extra hard once I was inside, partly to drown out her beautiful voice, and partly to let her know I was all done playing her game.

Chapter Two

Jogging the streets of Snowberry on a Sunday morning was the best time to think. Everyone was in church, and it resembled a ghost town as I ran up Main Street. I passed the Liberty Belle, Kiss's Café, and Savannah's Flower Emporium. The only thing open was the café, and I waved at April, who stood in the window, changing the morning specials. She waved back and I crossed the street, jogging toward home. It was early yet, but I couldn't sleep. The scene with Mandy Friday night bugged me so much that I spent the better part of the day at school yesterday, just to avoid running into her at home.

I couldn't figure the woman out. I'd been living next to her for five years. Sometimes she was friendly the way neighbors should be, and sometimes she acted like she wanted to kill me. Yet, at school, she was nothing but professional. My mind went back to Friday afternoon at school. She had never spoken to me that way before, and to be honest, it hurt a little bit. I wasn't her boss, at least on paper. Her boss, and the person who did all her observations and any disciplinary issues, was Neal

Newsom at the high school.

"Nice morning for a jog."

I turned my head to the left and saw Mandy riding her bike slowly on the street next to me.

"Or a bike ride," I answered, my breath coming in short puffs.

"I can't jog, my knees are bad," she explained, as though she needed an excuse. She was lying, though. It didn't roll off her tongue the way something that was true would. I shook my head. It must be my principal skills coming through.

"I should probably take up bike riding. I'm getting too old for this." I laughed a little, but she didn't.

"Hmm, didn't we just celebrate your thirty-fifth right before school got out?"

"Yeah, but that means I'm much closer to thirty-six now. I should probably start the paperwork for Snowberry Retirement Home."

She laughed and it was nice to hear something not covered in acid come out of her mouth. Her laugh was musical, much like the way she could make a piano sound when she played.

"Not a bad idea, you're creeping up there. I guess I better get an application, too. My kids think I'm ancient, after all."

"You're only thirty-four, you're not ancient, but you're getting there," I joked.

"How did you know I'm thirty-four? Did you look at my employment file?"

I shook my head. "Didn't need to. Ben told me.

I know everything there is to know about you, I think."

"Not everything," she murmured and then groaned, to cover it up. I pretended as if I didn't hear it when she went on with the conversation. "My son loves to talk, doesn't he?"

I laughed and nodded. "He sure does, but that's okay. He's incredibly smart and just likes to have someone to talk to who is interested in what he has to say."

It was as if a veil fell down over her face with my words and she picked up speed on her bike. "I better finish my ride. Have a nice day, Nick."

And like that, she was gone. I slowed my steps until I was walking and took a few deep breaths. I wiped the sweat off my face with my sleeve while she pedaled away. Something was going on with that woman and I was going to figure out what it was, even if it killed me. I laughed sardonically. It was possible she would be the one to kill me if I stuck my nose in where it didn't belong.

"Principal Klaus?" I looked up from my desk and saw my assistant standing in the doorway.

"Yes, Louis, did you need something?" I rose from my desk and he came in the door, holding the hand of one particular student who had never been in my office before.

"Mrs. Littlejohn sent Esther to see you. It seems she started a fight in class."

Esther stood with her head hanging low and I could hear her sniffing as Louis spoke. I approached them both and patted Louis on the shoulder. "Thanks, I'll take it from here."

"Do you want me to call her mom?" he asked, and I checked the clock.

"She's at the middle school right now and will be here in thirty. I'll talk to her then if need be."

He nodded and pulled the door closed behind him while I led Esther to a chair. I sat across from her, rather than behind my desk, so she didn't feel like I was judging her without hearing her side of the story.

"I've never seen you in my office before, Esther," I said, handing her a tissue.

"I'm sorry, Principal Klaus. I lost my cool," she whispered, swiping at her nose.

"Even if we lose our cool, we aren't allowed to punch someone."

She jerked her head up, shaking it hard. "I didn't punch anyone!"

"Okay, then explain to me why Mrs. Littlejohn thought you were fighting."

"Maybe it was because I yelled really loud and shoved Xander really hard."

"I'm inclined to think that's probably why, Esther. Want to tell me why you shoved Xander?"

She hung her head again and shook it. "No."

"If you don't tell me what happened, Esther, I'll have to call your mom in to talk about it."

She looked up, her eyes telling me how much she didn't want that to happen. "Please, don't bother my mom. She's already sad enough. I don't want her to be disappointed in me."

I leaned forward and rested my arms on my knees. "I don't think that would ever happen, but she probably would like to know why you're having a hard time in class."

"Because Xander is always picking on me!" she exclaimed, then clapped a tiny hand over her mouth.

"I see, and today you just got tired of it?"

She nodded, her hand falling from her mouth. "He was going to cut off my braid. He had his scissors and I shoved him so he wouldn't. I guess that wasn't very smart because he could have gotten hurt with scissors in his hand. Mrs. Littlejohn freaked out."

"Can't say that I blame her. Does she know why you shoved him?"

She shook her head no. "She didn't give me time to tell her. She just marched me right down here. Xander was smiling behind her back, too. I saw him."

"The next question that comes to mind is, why was Xander going to cut off your braid? He's not allowed to do that just like you aren't allowed to shove him."

"He said only old ladies are named Esther and

old ladies don't wear braids."

I sat back in the chair and could see this wasn't a one-time incident. "Has Xander been picking on you a lot?"

She nodded without looking at me. "Since Kindergarten."

"And you just started third grade, so it's been going on for …"

"Three years," she answered immediately.

"You know your math, little lady. Have you told anyone about this?"

"I told my kindergarten and first-grade teacher and they said boys will be like that."

"Boys will be boys, but that doesn't give them the right to pick on someone. Do you know why he picks on you?"

She shrugged one shoulder. "He says my name is stupid and that makes me stupid."

I didn't like this at all. Bullying was a situation we took very seriously in my school, and to have one of the teacher's kids taking the brunt of a bully was not going to go over well.

"You know that's not true, right?" I asked her and she shrugged one shoulder again.

"We don't allow bullying in our school, Esther. If Xander is causing a problem, then we will call him and his mom in here to talk about it."

She moaned and shook her head. "Please, don't. I promise not to get mad at him ever again. I'll just ignore him when he's mean to me."

"Why don't you want me to talk to Xander?"

"Because then he'll be even worse. Every time one of the teachers talks to him about being nice to me, he picks on me even more."

"Does he always pick on you about your name, or was that just what he was picking on you about today?"

"Always about my name, Principal Klaus, but this year he's started pushing me and pulling my hair."

I shook my head. "We can't have that, Esther."

"I don't know what to do about it. I've tried to be nice to him. I really have. I didn't want to shove him, but I got scared when he came at me with the scissors. I like my hair."

"I believe you, Esther. I would get scared, too, if someone was coming at me with scissors. I like your hair, too. It's very nice."

She captured the braid in her hand and held onto it like a lifeline. "I don't know what to do. I want to go home."

"Well, honey, you can't go home. We have to figure this out. Maybe we should put you in Mr. Lunden's class?"

"Xander will just pick on me at lunch and on the playground."

I shook my head. "I'm not going to allow this to go on any longer, Esther. This isn't your fault. He's the one with a problem and needs to change his attitude."

"Maybe I should just change my name. Maybe if they call me something else, he'll stop picking on me."

"Do you like your name?" I asked and she nodded.

"My mom named me after the girl in the Bible."

"Queen Esther, I presume?" I asked in a British accent.

She laughed at me and nodded. "That's her. Maybe I should read that part of the Bible now that I can read better."

"It probably would help you understand why it's such a cool name. Did you know that Esther is the woman who saved the Jewish people?" She shook her head no. "It's true, she did. She was a very strong and smart woman who figured out how to beat the men at their own game. Maybe you and I could read it together on the back patio if your mom will let you?"

"I would like that, Principal Klaus! Maybe it would teach me a way to beat Xander at his own game."

I laughed and shook my finger at her. "It just might, because you're also a smart girl."

I glanced up and saw Mandy breeze through the front doors. She came into the office to check-in, so I excused myself from Esther and left the office, approaching Mandy.

"Hey, Mandy, we have a bit of a problem."

She glanced up at me, surprised by the intrusion to her daily routine. "What kind of problem?"

"Esther is in my office. There was an incident in class."

One brow knitted and she put a hand on her hip. "My Esther?"

I chuckled. "She's the only Esther we have here."

"Esther doesn't have incidents."

"Did you know she's being bullied by a boy in class?"

The second hand went on her other hip. "She's not being bullied by anyone. If she was, she would have told me about it."

"She told me she didn't want to tell you because you're sad enough already."

Her shoulders slumped and she looked like someone had punched her in the gut. "I want to see her."

I crooked my finger and went to my office, holding the door open for her. Esther was in the chair, her head still hanging down while she stroked her braid.

I closed the door behind us, and Mandy grasped the little girl in her arms. "Esther, what happened? Principal Klaus said someone is being mean to you."

"I tried to take care of it by myself, mom, I really tried. Ben helped me last year with him, but now that he's at the middle school, I'm alone here and Xander knows it. This is only the second week of school and I don't ever want to come back," Esther cried.

Mandy rocked her in her arms lovingly. "I wish you hadn't kept it a secret, baby. Why didn't Ben tell me?"

Mandy sat in the chair I had vacated and held Esther's hand. "I told him if he did, I would tear up all his baseball cards."

"Esther!" Mandy scolded. "That's not appropriate."

"I know, but I didn't want him to tell you."

"Okay, we will talk about this later, at home. For now, we have to figure out what to do about Xander." She turned to me and waited.

"I agree. I was just telling Esther the first thing we should do is switch her to Mr. Lunden's room."

"Why should she have to change rooms? Shouldn't Xander be the one to leave?"

"If you would rather Esther stay in Mrs. Littlejohn's class, I can approach Xander's mom about switching him, but that will take time. She would also have to agree to it."

"I just don't think Esther should have to leave her friends because of one kid. Can't Mrs. Littlejohn do a better job of controlling the class?"

Esther tugged on her mom's arm. "Don't be mad at Mrs. Littlejohn. She doesn't know he does it. I don't tell anyone. It gets way worse after he's been scolded."

Mandy turned back to me and raised one brow. "In other words, the kid knows exactly what he's doing."

"It appears that way. I'll fight this any way you want to fight it, Mandy, but I won't let it go on any longer."

Mandy turned to her daughter. "Esther, you're in third grade now and you don't have to put up with this. I think you're old enough to be part of the decision. Do you want to move to the other class, or do you want to stay with Mrs. Littlejohn?"

"If I move, then Xander won't be mad about having to move and make things worse. At least if I'm in a different classroom, he can only pick on me at lunch and on the playground."

Mandy threw up her hands. "Why is he picking on her, anyway?"

"She told me he doesn't like her name," I answered in truth.

"Is that true, Esther?" she asked without taking her eyes off me.

"He says it's a name for old ladies," she whispered.

Mandy sighed. "Why are kids so mean?"

I gave her the palms up and shook my head with frustration. "Some parents don't teach their kids how to be kind. You're a teacher. You know the things we deal with on a daily basis."

She sighed heavily in response and Esther tugged on her mom's shirt again. "I would like to move to Mr. Lunden's class if he doesn't mind. I have a couple of friends in his class, so I won't be alone. It's only the second week of school and I shouldn't be too far behind them. I'll work extra hard to catch up."

I leaned over on my desk and addressed the girl. "Esther, Mr. Lunden teaches the same things

Mrs. Littlejohn does. You won't be behind if you move into his class. You don't have anything to worry about there."

She nodded and folded her hands. "Okay, then maybe that's for the best. I'll just have to avoid Xander at recess and at lunch."

Mandy shook her head. "No, you won't have to avoid him. You'll tell an adult if he's bothering you and he'll be held accountable for his behavior. I will make that very clear in the meeting we will be having with Xander and his mother."

Esther groaned loudly. "Do you have to?" Mandy nodded, and Esther grimaced. "Do I have to be there?"

Mandy pulled her daughter into a hug and kissed the top of her head. "No, you don't have to be there. You didn't do anything wrong."

Esther looked up at her mom. "Yes, I did. I shoved Xander today while he had scissors in his hands. He could have gotten hurt."

"Why did you shove him?"

"He was threatening to cut off my braid. He said old ladies don't have braids."

Mandy looked to me for help and I shook my head for lack of anything else to do. "I know this has to be dealt with. Our district has a firm line on bullying. It's not tolerated, but if we don't know it's happening, we can't stop it. It appears Esther told her teachers in kindergarten and first grade, but they didn't bring it to me. That will be remedied. For now, we need to get Esther back to class. She won't be reprimanded for the incident today. She was protecting herself. While she shouldn't have shoved him, I'm confident she knows that without me punishing her, in light of the bigger picture."

Esther nodded her head solemnly and looked down at her hands. "I apologized before Mrs. Littlejohn dragged me out of the room."

Mandy snorted and I bit the inside of my lip to keep from laughing. I picked up the phone and punched in an extension. When Mr. Lunden answered the phone, I explained the situation. He was on board and I hung up, gazing up at two anxious faces.

"Mr. Lunden would love for you to come to his class. He has a spare desk and was wondering who would fill it, so I say we get your things from Mrs. Littlejohn's room and get you settled."

"Thank you, Principal Klaus," she said, relieved. "Can we wait a few minutes until recess, though? I don't want Xander to see me leaving with my tail between my legs."

Mandy took her daughter's shoulders firmly. "You are an Alexander, young lady, and we never walk away with our tail between our legs. Do you understand me?" Esther nodded, grimacing a little at her mother's tone. "You're being the better person here by not insisting Xander be removed from the class. That's what Alexander women do. You should be proud of that."

Esther nodded again. "Okay, Mom, but I still want to wait until recess."

I looked up at the clock. "That's only a few minutes, sweetie. Why don't you go sit with Louis for a few minutes while I talk to your mom privately? When the bell rings, I'll go with you and get you settled in Mr. Lunden's room."

Esther jumped down off the chair and her mom hugged her one more time before she left the room. I clicked the door closed behind her and steeled myself for what was about to happen.

"I cannot believe this has been going on since kindergarten and no one stopped it!" Mandy exclaimed.

And here we go.

"As I told Esther, I will deal with that, Mandy. You know I do not allow bullying in this school. You've seen the line I've drawn in the sand about it, and that I'm not afraid to enforce it, haven't you?"

She sat back down in her chair and let out a breath, though her hands were still in fists. "I know. I'm sorry. It's just that she's so sweet and he's picking on her because of her name? And his name is Xander, no less!"

I held up my hand. "I have a feeling this has a lot less to do with her name and more to do with the fact that she's a teacher's kid. If I was a betting man, I would guess that's the reason Xander chose her as his victim."

"That doesn't even make sense, Nick. What does being a teacher's kid have anything to do with this?"

"In my experience, other kids think teacher's

kids get preferential treatment."

"But they don't! It's usually harder for a teacher's kid. It's as though they start the year with a knock against them already."

I sat on the edge of my desk and swung my leg. "While I'm aware of that, Mandy, many parents believe it to be true. Their kids hear them talking and think every teacher's kid is getting a free pass, and we both know that's not the case. I can't change that preconceived notion, but I can change how their child behaves in this school."

"What are we going to do?" she asked finally, her anger gone.

"Well, you're going to go teach the second graders how to play the xylophone while I get Esther situated in her new class."

She shook her head. "No, I'll do that. I'm her mother."

I crossed my arms. "Exactly, you're her mother and the music teacher. If you're not teaching the second graders, who is? I'll have to send Louis down to cover your class and he can't carry a tune in a bushel basket." She looked confused and I pointed toward the door of my office. "My point here, Mandy, is that if the kids see you hustling Esther into Mr. Lunden's room, they *are* going to think she is getting preferential treatment. That will only reinforce what they already believe. If I'm the one getting her settled, the kids will think this was my decision and they will sympathize with Esther and her plight."

Mandy rubbed her forehead and nodded. "Okay, I guess I see what you mean."

"After I get her settled, Xander's parents will be called. If one of them can't come in and talk to me immediately, Xander will be eating lunch and doing his studies with me until they can. I won't put him back out there until he, and his parents, are fully aware of the consequences if he continues to pick on Esther."

"I want to be there for that meeting," she said, but I shook my head.

"That's not going to happen, Mandy, and I'll tell you why. First of all, you're a hothead and you yell and flail your arms around without thinking, at least when it comes to your children. Second of all, I want to make it *very* clear to them that I'm the one bringing this world of hurt down on them, not you. If you're in the room, they're going to think you're forcing me to say what I'm going to say. That undermines both of our effectiveness, not just for me, but for you in the classroom. You have Xander in music class, no?"

She nodded and crossed her arms. "I do, and he's a real pain in the butt there, too, but I've never seen him picking on anyone."

"Do you understand why I'm doing things the way I am?" I asked.

She stood and picked up her bag. "I do, and as much as I want to be in this room yelling and flailing my arms around, I understand it's better if I'm not. I trust I will be informed of what is agreed upon at the meeting?"

"Of course, but the answer to that is simple. Xander will comply, or he will not be allowed to come to school."

"I'm worried about Esther. Maybe I should take her home and let her rest for the day."

I stood and took her arm, guiding her to my door. "She's an Alexander, and an Alexander woman doesn't run with her tail between her legs."

She laughed a little, but I knew she got my point. I opened the door and Esther sat on the chair next to Louis as they played something on an iPad.

"All right, little lady, the bell is about to ring, so let's go on down and talk to Mrs. Littlejohn while your mom heads to class."

Esther thanked Louis for the game and joined us by the door. She hugged her mom for a quick second, whispering in her ear, "I'll be okay, Mom. Please don't worry."

Mandy straightened her braid and tucked a piece of hair back in the rubber band. "I'm not worried. I know you'll be fine. Say hi to Mr. Lunden for me."

Mandy walked away quickly, the emotions she was feeling etched on her face. I felt terrible for making her leave, but this was necessary if Esther's torture was ever going to come to an end. I put my hand on Esther's shoulder and gave her an encouraging smile as we walked toward the third-grade hallway.

Chapter Three

I stepped from the shower and grabbed my towel, tying it around my waist. What an incredibly long day that turned out to be. By the time I finished addressing the issues with Xander, it was well after six and I still had to wrap up my end of day work. It was seven-thirty now and I intended to enjoy a drink on the back patio while I grilled a steak for dinner.

I threw on a pair of sweats and a Snowberry Bears t-shirt, then grabbed a beer and headed for the grill. I could almost taste the prime cut of meat melting on my tongue. I slid the patio doors open and stepped out, the darkness already steeped in for the night. I longed for the days of summer when it was still bright out at nine. I lifted the lid on the grill and reached for the igniter knob when I heard, "God, what am I going to do?"

I froze and listened in the night air for more, but all I heard was the sound that could only be one thing, crying. It was quiet as if she was trying to be sneaky, but my neighbor likely didn't know I had ears like an owl. I went back through the patio doors and grabbed a second beer from the fridge. I looked longingly at the steak. The sane side of me said, *Go about fixing it and don't worry about her.* The glutton for punishment side of me was the one who pushed through the bushes on the property line.

"Mandy?" I called, not wanting to scare her.

When I came out of the trees, the dim light showed me one frantic woman, swiping at her face and scrambling under a blanket.

"I don't want company, Nick," she growled at me and her voice was raw and raspy.

I held a beer out to her. "How about a beer then?"

She hesitated, but finally took it from my hand and brought it to her overheated cheek. The chill of the bottle seemed to settle her. I sat in the chair opposite her and took a drink from my own bottle.

"It's a nice night out," I said to make conversation.

"I guess," she answered, screwing the lid off the bottle and taking a sip.

"I heard you crying."

"I didn't think it was against the law to cry in my own backyard. My apologies."

"I didn't say it was against the law. I said I heard you crying."

She shrugged and took another swig of the beer. "I thought I was being quiet."

I tapped the beer bottle on the metal frame of the chair a couple times. I didn't want to start a fight with her, but finding her crying seemed to be a theme lately, and I wanted to know why. "You were being quiet, but I have ears like an owl, or maybe a bat." I rolled my eyes at myself and took a breath. "Basically, I hear just about everything. It can be a real annoyance at times, but my sisters used to pay me to listen in on each other's conversations."

"You have sisters?" she asked, obviously happy to steer the conversation away from herself.

"Yup, three of them, all older. I didn't stand a chance of not being used as a pawn."

"I have four brothers, Jake, Dully, Jay, and finally, Bram."

"Bram, he's the photographer, right? Just married Liberty?"

She nodded. "Well, if by *just* you mean almost a year ago next week, then yes."

"Wow, has it been that long?" I shook my head. "Time flies."

"It sure does. It seems like yesterday my own kids were just babies. Now even Dully's babies aren't babies anymore. Jo-Jo is eighteen months and, well, you know Sunny."

I laughed easily. "Oh, boy, do I know Sunny. She's quite the little girl. You gotta love her, though. She doesn't take garbage from anyone."

"Maybe Esther should take some lessons from her," she said, resigned.

"Mands, what happened with Esther and Xander wasn't her fault. She wasn't provoking him to be mean to her."

"I know, and thanks, by the way, for getting her settled in Mr. Lunden's class. He stopped in after school to let me know he put her next to her friends for a few days until she feels comfortable. I know she'll do fine."

"That's my job and I take it very seriously. I met with Xander and his mom today after school."

"How did that go?"

"Not surprisingly, Xander's mom didn't know anything about it. She was less than pleased to be called in, and then to find out it had been going on for years."

"Hmm, so what happened?"

"For starters, she took away every piece of electronic equipment he owns, or so she tells me, and decided he would be reading the book of Esther to start off since he was so narrowminded as to think it was an *old lady name*." Which I put in quotes like his mother did at the time.

"I guess it kind of is. I mean, to most kids anyway. I didn't think it was when I named her that."

"You don't have to defend your choice of names, Mandy. Esther is a wonderful name for a girl. She could do much worse than having Queen Esther as a role model."

She shrugged. "I guess so. When I got pregnant the first time, we decided I would name the girl and he would name the boy. He chose Benjamin, but he thought out the possible nicknames. I didn't do that when I named Esther. I'm a teacher, I should have."

"Why are you sitting here beating yourself up for giving your child a name that has served her well so far? The fact that she's named Esther has nothing to do with why Xander is picking on her any more than the fact that you're named Mandy."

She threw her hands up, sloshing the beer over the side of the bottle. "Then why is he picking on her?"

"I'm glad you asked," I said, knowing I was probably poking the bear, but I was enjoying the conversation. "He's been picking on her because his stepdad picked on him. His mom left his stepdad, but the damage has been done."

She hung her head. "Crap, I had no idea."

"Neither did I, Mands, so don't feel bad. I think his mom is just a little out of her depth right now."

"I know the feeling," she muttered, but I let it go, for now.

"He's going to be seeing the school psychologist for the next few months until he gets a handle on his feelings. In the meantime, he knows he's supposed to stay away from Esther. His mom told him if he so much as looks at her wrong, he won't have his gadgets back for a year. Of course, we won't tell Esther that."

She laughed and shook her head. "Knowing Esther, once she finds out Xander is hurting, she'll be the one who goes out of her way to be nice to him."

"That must be the Alexander gene in her." She looked up and I winked, trying to smooth over the rough day we both had.

"What is that supposed to mean?"

I forced myself not to roll my eyes at the woman. She could go from zero to defensive faster than a fighter jet. "I mean the Alexanders are notably the kindest family in this town. She's grown up with what I can only imagine to be a very healthy dose of empathy towards those who aren't always treated kindly."

She sipped at her beer. "I suppose you're right there. Well, thanks for letting me know what happened. Have a good night, Nick."

"All of that being worked out, it doesn't explain why I've found you crying twice in as many weeks."

She twirled the bottle around in the air, trying to think of a way out of answering my question.

"Being a parent isn't always easy, Nick. It's the beginning of the school year and I'm stressed out."

"I don't imagine being a working parent is easy, no less a single working parent."

"Jacob is still part of their lives."

I glanced around. "I don't see him here every day. How often do they see him?"

"Every other weekend and a few weeks in the summer. Less than that, it seems, the older they get."

"Then I stand by my opinion that being a single parent is hard."

"Some days are harder than others, especially now that Ben is in middle school. Things are …. stressful, right now and I hope that settles down soon, but in the meantime, I just have to take it day by day."

"And cry when they aren't around or in bed, so they don't hear you and think it's their fault?"

She shrugged but nodded. "I guess that's accurate."

"Mom?"

I turned and Ben stood on the patio watching us. I motioned him over and he tiptoed through the grass in his bare feet until he reached his mother.

He hugged her rather suddenly. "I'm sorry for being a jerk and talking back. I thought about what you said and you were right. Please don't cry."

She hugged him and I tried not to notice her chin trembling at his words. "It's okay, Ben, we'll work through this together, just like we always have."

He pulled back and wiped a tear away from her face that had fallen. For a fifth-grader, he was far too observant. "If you believe that, how come you're still crying?"

She hung her head and I stood, putting my hand on his shoulder and leading him back to the house. "Sometimes moms cry, Ben. They have a lot on their plate and from time-to-time, it feels a little overwhelming. It's no one's fault."

He stopped at the door to the patio and glanced around me at his mother. "I shoulda told her about Esther."

"Let me tell you a secret about life, Ben.

Shoulda, woulda, and coulda are all useless words because we only use them after the fact. Now that all of this is out in the open use what happened as a lesson the next time something comes up that you aren't sure what to do. If you think you should do something, then you're most likely right."

He looked up at me and nodded. "You give good advice, Principal Klaus, thanks."

I pulled the door open and nodded. "You're welcome, but now that you're in middle school, I think you can just call me Nick, okay?"

"Okay, night, Nick," he said a bit uncomfortable, and I waved.

"Night, Ben." I leaned in and whispered my next words. "If your mom is crying and you don't know why, you know where to find me, 'kay?" I gave him a wink and he gave me a little salute before heading for his room.

I turned and went back to the small fire pit and patted her on the shoulder. "He'll be fine, Mands."

She shrugged. "Sometimes I wonder how not having a male presence in his life every day will affect him as he gets older."

"He's got your dad, all his uncles, and his father. Maybe they aren't here every day, but he has some solid male role models in his life to emulate."

She tipped the bottle back and drained it. When it was empty, she tipped it toward me. "Yeah, I guess. I better head in and get them ready for bed. Thanks for the beer, and the chat."

"Anytime, Mandy."

She was definitely dismissing me and the sane part of me said it was time to leave while I was still on her good side. We had a friendly conversation that didn't involve much yelling. That was a start. I headed for the lot line and stopped without turning back.

"Are the kids with their dad this coming weekend?" I asked over my shoulder.

"They go there after school on Friday and I pick them up on Sunday," she answered.

"Next weekend is the fall fest in town. Why don't we go and enjoy the band? Maybe a little time without the kids is what you need."

"That's probably not a good idea, Nick. How would that look? You're my boss, after all."

"Actually, Neal is your boss. I'm simply the principal in one of the schools you work in. To answer your question, I would think it would look like two colleagues who live in the same town enjoying their community since that's all it would be. People do that all the time."

"I suppose you're right."

"No, I am right. Now, would you like to go to the band Friday night with me? You can even bring one of your brothers along to chaperone if you feel the need."

She laughed, which was a far better sound than her crying. "I don't feel the need, though chances are one or all of them will be there."

"I can accept that. I enjoy chatting with Dully. He always has a great story to share."

"I'll be ready at seven?"

I turned back and noticed she had a slight smile on her face. "I'll pick you up then."

Before she could change her mind, I pushed my way back through the bushes and did a fist pump when my feet hit my patio.

Chapter Four

"I'm bummed that it decided to pour this weekend after such a long dry spell," Mandy lamented over her drink.

"Me, too. I was really looking forward to kicking back and relaxing with some good tunes and great company," I agreed. "The good news is, you came to dinner with me anyway, and the event will be back on next weekend. Maybe we could take the kids to the fire hose competition since they'll be home."

"They would like that a lot. I'm sure you've noticed they think very highly of you."

I shrugged. "They're great kids, Mands. You should be proud of the job you're doing raising them."

She set her drink down. "It bugs the crap out of me when you call me Mands."

"Why?" I asked.

She took a long drink of her Long Island iced tea before she answered. "I don't know."

I raised my brow. "If you don't know, then it really shouldn't bother you."

She leaned forward on the table and glared at

me. "I don't like how familiar it sounds rolling off your tongue."

"Now, that's an answer I can deal with, Mands."

She held her hands up. "Okay, you know what? Forget it, Nicholas, call me Mands all you want."

"Thanks, I will. You probably shouldn't call me Nicholas, though, I won't answer. My real name is Nick. Sorry-not-sorry."

"Your parents didn't give you a full name? That's harsh."

I laughed, shaking my head. "What's wrong with Nick? My full name is Nick S. Klaus, Jr."

Her brow went up. "Oh, so you're a junior? I guess the blame for your name falls on your grandparents then."

"It's hard to name your kid Nicholas when his last name is Klaus."

"So instead they went with Nick? I'm not seeing much improvement there."

I gave her the palms up and took a drink of my beer. "Take it up with my grandparents. They were German, that's all I got."

"Where do your parents live now?" she asked conversationally.

"God's Acre Cemetery, Saxony Germany."

She set her glass down very slowly. "I'm sorry, Nick, I thought you all lived here in the States now. Were both your parents German?"

"No, my mom was American. She was teaching for the DOD when she met my dad. He was German."

She laughed freely and accepted her plate from the waitress, who set a pile of mozzarella sticks in the middle of the table and went back to the kitchen.

She dipped a stick in marinara sauce and eyed me. "So, you have dual citizenship?"

"I do, though I moved to the US and finished my senior year of high school here. I didn't want to register for the service in Germany when I turned eighteen. You don't always get a choice over there about serving in the military the way you do here. I knew I wanted to be a teacher and I wanted to go to college here, not over there."

"Do all of your sisters live here, too?"

"No, only one sister lives in the States. She's out in San Francisco. My other two stayed in Germany because they each married a German. They come once a year and we all meet up in San Fran over spring break."

"Why did your sister choose San Francisco if you're here?" she asked while I dipped a mozzarella stick in marinara.

"My sister, Cara, is gay and she lives there with her wife. She's the head of a nonprofit organization and her wife is an RN." Her mouth was open in a perfect O and I chuckled. "Makes sense now, right?"

"Yeah, sorry, I shouldn't ask so many questions."

"Don't apologize. I don't mind answering them. Cara moved here and met her wife, Sandy, the first week. She dropped a loaded box on her arm and had to go to the ER."

She laughed softly. "She sounds about as graceful as I am."

"She's an expert skier, but can't walk without tripping. I'm glad she's closer than Germany, and she's safer here."

"I guess Germany isn't as forward-thinking about the LGBTQ community as we are."

I swallowed my cheese stick and washed it down with some beer. "Not so much. It's better than it used to be, but Cara always felt like she was on guard. I encouraged her to move here and make a better life for herself. We miss my sisters and their kids, but I didn't want to see Cara unhappy any longer."

She patted my hand. "You're a good brother."

"When my parents died, I kind of felt like I was the one left to look after her. My other sisters were married already by the time they passed, but Cara was over there and I was here. It was hard to take care of her from that kind of distance."

"So why Snowberry? Why not California?" she asked as the waitress arrived with our pizza.

Gallo's pizza was the best in town and the place was busy as it usually was on a Friday night. We were tucked away in a back booth, not paying attention to anyone around us. I was thoroughly enjoying myself and hoped she was, too.

I served her a piece of Gallo's signature pizza then put one slice on my plate while the waitress went to refill our drinks.

"My grandparents, my mom's parents, lived in St. Paul, so when I came over to finish high school, I lived with them. My grandfather died the first year I was in college and my grandmother the last. My mom was much older when she had us kids, so my grandparents were in their late eighties when they passed away. I liked the Midwest and had no time for the hassles of big cities. I taught in St. Paul for two years and as soon as I got my license for administration, I started applying in every small school district in Minnesota."

She laid her pizza down and took a sip of her drink. "I guess Snowberry lucked out then. You're the best principal the elementary school has seen, not to mention the longest-running."

"I've only been here five years," I pointed out and she nodded.

"Like I said, the longest-running. We don't have much luck keeping teachers or principals in this town."

"I don't understand why. This is a great little town and the people in it are wonderful. Salt of the earth kind of people."

She nodded, chewing, so I took a bite of my own. The cheese was salty and the anchovies were just the right touch. Gallo's was famous for their sun-dried tomato, mozzarella, and anchovy pizza.

She wiped her hands on her napkin and nodded. "That's the problem. We might be too salt of the earth. Young people get bored and move on to greener pastures. I've lived here all my life, but people who come in from bigger cities tend to move away once they get some teaching experience here."

"I can see that. The sidewalks do roll up about nine around here every night, but I like that about this town. Crime is low and friendliness is high. There's nothing wrong with staying in a small town if it makes you happy. I spent enough time in a big city to know it wasn't for me."

We ate in companionable silence for a bit, each lost in our own thoughts. The restaurant was getting too loud to carry on a conversation by the time we finished our pizza, so I motioned the waitress over and she brought our check.

"Here, let me get that," she said over the din, but I waved her away, handing the waitress some cash and telling her to keep the change. I stood and grabbed Mandy's coat from the hook by the booth and helped her on with it. We didn't speak again until we were outside in the silence of the night.

"Wow, that place was loud," I said, the ringing in my ears making my head hurt. It was raining, and I popped the umbrella up, holding it over our heads as we walked.

"It sure was. I guess the rain drove everyone inside," she said as she tipped into me.

I righted her again and glanced at her, concerned. "Are you sure you're okay to walk home?"

She nodded, but I noticed with each step she grimaced when she stepped down on her left foot.

By the time we made it to our block, she couldn't take another step.

"Did you hurt yourself?" I asked when we paused. She was eyeing the curbs hesitantly.

"I think I have a blister or something. I'm in pain."

I handed her the umbrella and bent down, scooping her up. I carried her to the door and set her back on her feet, keeping my arm around her waist. She unlocked the door, limped in, and collapsed onto the couch in a heap.

I folded the umbrella and set it next to the door to drip off. "What can I do to help?"

She waved me away with her hand. "Nothing, I'll be fine. Thanks for dinner. I really appreciate the company with the kids gone."

I sat opposite her on the ottoman. "You're welcome for dinner and I appreciate the company as well. It gets lonely being the guy no one wants to be seen with."

She half-laughed and I smiled, happy to have made her laugh at least once tonight. "That's not true, it's just most people are too intimidated to hang out with their principal."

"I'm glad you're not. Now, how about if you explain to me why your legs clank together when they touch."

She grimaced and looked anywhere but at me. "They don't clank."

"Yes, they clanked when I picked you up. Add that to the fact that you walk funny, which I always just thought was a knee problem, and I think there's a part of the picture I'm missing here."

She didn't say anything but pulled her pants legs up slowly.

I was stunned silent by what I saw. "Are those braces?" I asked, trying to understand.

She shook her head, "No, they're prosthesis. I don't have feet."

"You don't have feet?" I parroted and she bent and took off her shoes.

"I don't have feet. They were both amputated at the ankle."

I sat back as though I had been slapped, staring at the plastic and metal feet, the toes pointing straight up into the air. "I had no idea, Mandy."

"Only the people I grew up with know. I would like to keep it that way."

"Why?" I asked perplexed.

"I don't show them to people."

"That doesn't answer my question, Mandy."

"They're the reason my husband left me, okay?" she shouted, her voice going up an octave, but in perfect pitch. She lowered her voice and spoke again before I could. "Now, if you'll excuse me, I need to take these off and find out what's wrong."

"I don't think I should leave you here alone if you're hurt," I said carefully.

"I'm not hurt. This happens a lot. I know I need new legs, but I've been putting it off. Looks like I can't put it off any longer."

"Why have you been putting it off?" I asked, surprised. "We have good benefits at school."

"We do, but I still have to pay twenty percent. On two of these, that's about four thousand dollars."

"Oh, wow," I said in surprise. "I guess I can see why you put it off."

She motioned at them. "I won't need feet this time since these are still in good shape. Maybe that will help some. I might get away with three thousand. I can't work if I can't walk, so I'll have to do it now." I was trying not to smile and she noticed. "What?"

I held my hand up. "Sorry, the whole *I won't need feet because these are still in good shape* was kind of funny."

She lowered one brow, but even she started to smile. In seconds, we were both laughing outright. "I guess that does sound a little funny to someone who isn't used to it."

"Okay, what do we need to do in order to help you walk better until you can go see your doctor?"

"Well, that depends on what I find inside the legs when I take them off."

I motioned at them. "Don't let me stop you."

Her eyes widened and she shook her head. "No, I'm not taking them off in front of you. You can go, really, I'll be fine."

"Mands, really, as if I'm just going to leave you here in pain while I go home and pretend you're fine. That's not going to happen. You might as well know that right now."

"I don't want you to see them," she whispered again, but I refused to budge.

"And I don't want you to be hurt. What do you think is going to happen, Mandy? I'm going to run screaming from the room. Give me a little credit."

"Okay, your funeral," she said as she pulled two Velcro straps and removed a backplate from the first leg. She pulled her leg from the brace by tabs. She did the same to the second leg and then reattached the removable plate, setting the legs aside. "I can walk on the ends of my limbs because the ankle bone is still there," she explained as she rolled the liner off. Her legs were almost matchstick thin at the bottom, except for a bulbous knob at the end. Her right side was fine, but her left side was not.

She held the liner in one hand and the other hand under her leg, which was dripping blood off the end. "Could you get me some paper towels from the kitchen?" she asked, motioning toward the other room with her chin. "They're under the sink."

I jumped up and ran into the kitchen to grab the roll. I felt helpless, so I was glad I had something I could do. When I came back, she had rolled the liner so it was extended again and the blood was trapped inside. She took the paper towels in one hand and held the liner out to me. "Could you set that in the kitchen sink just like that?"

I took the top of the liner and carried it in carefully, taking a little extra time to wash the blood out before I laid it in the sink for her to take care of later. When I came back into the living room, she was dabbing at the end of the leg with the paper towel. Every time she touched it, she flinched.

I squatted down and took a better look. The skin was completely gone over the bottom in a circle the size of a quarter, and you could see all the way through to the flesh. "I think you need to see a doctor."

"It will have to wait until morning now. It's too late, and I don't know anyone who makes house calls."

She leaned her head back on the couch after resting her leg on the paper towel and I grabbed her phone, happy to find what I was looking for immediately. She sat up when I brought the phone to my ear.

"Hey, what are you doing?" she yelled, but I ignored her when the phone was picked up.

"Hi, Mrs. Alexander?" I asked.

"Yes, who is this? Why are you calling me from Mandy's number?"

"This is her next-door neighbor, Nick Klaus. I'm with Mandy at her house and she has an open and bleeding sore on her left leg. I think a doctor should look at it before morning."

I heard her repeat the conversation to someone else in the room and then came back to the phone. "She let you look at her leg?" she asked, her voice holding a tinge of awe.

"I didn't really give her a choice, ma'am. She was having a hard time walking and I wanted to know why. It's bleeding profusely and there is no skin over the spot on the bottom. She's rubbed it away."

"'Tom says to take her to the ER," she said, then the line went dead.

She folded her arms and huffed at me. "You did not just call my daddy."

I tossed the phone back down on the couch. "I did, as a matter of fact. You know you can't let that go until morning, and while I respect your stubbornness, I need you at school. None of the substitute teachers can carry a tune or play the piano."

She shook her head and lay it back on the couch pillow. "Dammit, I don't need this right now, of all times. Things are bad enough."

She started to cry again and I felt like a fish out of water. I knelt next to her and held her hand, patting it comfortingly. I didn't want her to cry, not because it made me uncomfortable, but because I hated seeing her so sad.

"Is something going on that I don't know about, Mandy? Is there something going on at work that you don't want to bring to Neal or me?"

She shook her head. "No, everything is fine at school."

"I'm going to let this go for now because your dad said to take you to the ER. I guess we better get you ready."

She sighed and the tears stopped at the mention of her father. "Of course, he did. Forget it. I'll clean it up myself and call my doc in the morning. It can wait a few more hours. This isn't my first rodeo."

"Mandy, I don't think you should wait. What if it's infected?"

"I have antibiotics in my cupboard. I'm already ahead of you."

There was a knock on the door and I glanced at her, surprised. "I thought he wasn't coming. Are you expecting anyone?" She shook her head no. "I'll get it, don't move," I ordered.

"Where am I going to go?" she called as I opened the door.

Standing on the doorstep was a very anxious-looking woman. "Nick," she said in surprise. "I wasn't expecting you to be here.

"Hi, December," I greeted Mandy's sister-in-law, who pushed her way in. "Mandy can't come to the door right now."

"I know. Jay sent me over to look at her leg."

"Oh, I'm relieved. She's refusing to go to the ER."

December shrugged out of her coat and I took it, hanging it on the closet doorknob. "I'm sure she is, not that I blame her. I work in the ER and I don't want to go there."

I laughed and she followed me into the living room where Mandy was still on the couch, still dabbing at the wound with a paper towel.

"Hey, sis, I heard you had a wardrobe malfunction," December said, crossing the room to where Mandy sat.

I could see Mandy's shoulders visibly relax when she heard December's voice. "Hi, December, I'm sorry Nick dragged you out of the house so late."

"I wasn't at home. I was in my car heading home when Jay called me. I guess he heard what Suzie told Tom and knew you wouldn't go to the hospital. He asked me to stop here on my way home."

Mandy smiled at her sister-in-law and gave her a little fist bump. "Jay would be the one to understand not wanting to go to the ER. I don't know what happened. We went to the fall fest, and on the way home, I had trouble walking. I guess the busy week back to school caused a blister and it popped. Nick helped me in."

December stood with her finger in the air and opened her mouth, then closed it, then opened it, confusion contorting her face. "But Fall fest was canceled until next weekend."

I jumped in. "It was, but she had already agreed to go with me. I've been working for five years to get her to do anything social in the grownup world, so I took her to Gallo's, and we walked home from there. That's when the problem occurred."

December snickered and shook her finger at me. "I like you. You can stay." Then she turned to Mandy and knelt down, inspecting the leg.

"How long have you been walking on it like

this?" she asked her, pulling a flashlight from her scrubs pocket and aiming it at the wound.

"It's been a problem spot for a few weeks, but I was treating it right. I'm not sure what happened today."

"I think the tissue was swelling and you didn't know it. Most likely, it formed a blister that popped as soon as you put enough friction against it. You're going to have to stay off it for the weekend, if not longer. I'm going to clean it out and bandage it. You still have antibiotics here?"

"Yep, I'll start them tonight."

"And the kids are with Jacob, right?"

Mandy nodded and leaned her head back again. "I'm supposed to pick them up on Sunday."

"I'll go pick them up on Sunday," December said quickly. "After dinner, I'll bring them back here for you. It's best to give that as much time to heal as you can. It will be important to put it up and keep the swelling down."

"That would be great if you could pick them up, December. I have Tegaderm here. If I use that, it will heal in a couple days," she insisted.

"If you stay off it," December scolded.

"I'll give her Monday and Tuesday off," I said, and they stared at me as though they forgot I was in the room.

Mandy shook her head. "No, I will need my sick days for trips to Rochester to get the new legs made. I'll come to school but use my crutches. Touchdown weight-bearing will be okay by then.

I'll just tell the kids I hurt my ankle over the weekend."

"You're getting a little ahead of yourself. I'll be the judge on Sunday night as to whether you'll be going to school on Monday." December stopped speaking and frowned. "Wait a minute, does Jacob know you need new legs?"

Mandy grimaced, shaking her head. "No, he doesn't, and I would prefer it to stay that way."

December turned to me. "Would you help me get her to the bedroom?"

I nodded and bent down, slipping my arms under Mandy's legs and back, then curling her into me. I smiled down at her and she closed her eyes, clearly embarrassed, but knowing she didn't have a choice. I followed December through the house and down the hall, each step bringing me closer to the space I had dreamed about so many times. Mandy Alexander's bedroom. I swallowed hard, kept the smile plastered on my face, and entered the room. One glance across the space and the only way I could describe it was simply, Mandy.

There were images of musicians on the walls done in black and white but held in colorful frames. The furniture was simple, understated and soft oak in color. The dresser had a mirror and I saw myself reflected in it. I was holding Mandy close to me, her head tucked into my shoulder as though she trusted me with her life. The image would forever be burned into my memory and was one I would cherish, even if I never held her in my arms again.

December pulled the music note comforter down and I settled Mandy onto the bed. She surprised me when I went to move my hand and she grabbed it. She held it for no more than a few seconds, but it was long enough to say thank you without words.

"Would you go rustle up an icepack?" December asked, gathering supplies from the master bath. I'm going to get this cleaned up and she's going to need ice when I'm done with it."

I nodded my head once and turned toward the kitchen, thankful I didn't have to watch what she was about to do.

Chapter Five

I settled her in against her pillows and pulled up a chair next to her bed. "Feeling any better?" I asked and she did the so-so hand.

"I didn't think it would hurt that bad. Good thing you moved fast with that wastebasket or my bedroom carpet would be wearing Gallo's pizza."

"Hey, that's part of the job. You get puked on once by a kid and you learn to move quick with the garbage can."

She laughed, but I could hear the fatigue in her voice. "True story. I still remember my first time like it was yesterday."

I rubbed her arm up and down soothingly. "I'm glad your sister-in-law thinks this will heal quickly, but I still want you to take it easy. If you insist on coming to school, then I'll insist you use your crutches, at least while you're in my building."

She held up her hand. "No worries, I'll use them. I don't have a choice if this is going to heal, and I need it to heal before I can get new castings made."

"Why did December ask if your ex knew you

needed new ones?" I asked cautiously.

"Probably because he's supposed to pay for them," she answered, shifting on the bed into a more comfortable position.

"Because?"

"Because it's his fault I'm a bilateral amputee. The terms of the divorce were that he paid the deductible portion of the prostheses as long as I carried insurance on myself."

"Is that why you got divorced? Because of this?" I asked, pointing at her legs.

She laughed and leaned her head back, closing her eyes. "No, this happened when we were kids. Well, I was nineteen and he was twenty-one. We were out for the night, partying, drinking, and dancing. He got mad at me because I told him he needed to quit drinking. I wasn't legal drinking age, but I also couldn't drive a stick shift. He decided to show me he wasn't too drunk to drive and challenged another guy to a race. I was trying to get him to stop and he ran over me with his truck. Both feet were crushed and all the doctors could do was amputate at the ankle. If the same thing happened today, I would probably be a below the knee amputee, but Snowberry is a small hospital. They tried to save what they could, so they took the shattered bones off and left me with my ankles."

"Geez, Mandy, I'm sorry," I said, knowing it was lame, but not knowing what else to say. How do you comfort someone whose life was changed because of someone else?

"It was my fault. He was drunk and I should have been smarter about where I was standing."

I shook my head. "No, it wasn't your fault. It was his fault for drinking and being a showoff. I had my fair share of drunken parties, but I made sure no one drove home."

She shrugged. "Needless to say, my dad was not pleased with Jacob after that. I healed and we stayed together. I got my teaching degree and Jacob finished seminary."

"Ahh," I said, snapping my fingers.

"What?"

"The Bible names were confusing me, now it makes sense. Benjamin is the last son of Jacob."

She nodded. "Yeah, it made sense to name him Benjamin. I loved the name Esther and I felt like maybe she was going to be what saved our marriage."

"Sorry for interrupting," I said. "Go on."

"Not much more to say. We got married and within a year had Benjamin and then a couple years later, we had Esther. Jacob always promised he would never stop loving me, but I guess he was wrong. Somehow, someway, he stopped loving me. When we got divorced, the judge ordered Jacob to pay for my care the way anyone who caused an accident like that would. He barely got probation after the initial accident since I refused to file charges, and it was his first offense. That said, he didn't pay for the last set of legs, I did."

"Why don't you make him?" I asked, confused.

"He barely pays his child support, Nick. How do you squeeze blood from a turnip? He's a pastor for a small church and has to pay his own expenses. There's only so much to go around."

"How long have you been divorced?" I asked, leaning back in the chair and stretching out my legs.

"Almost six years now. He was working in Rochester at the time, so I worked here and then picked up the kids at daycare. I got done early one day due to a snowstorm and when I got home, his car was in the driveway. I was happy he beat the storm home until I walked in and found him naked with another woman in the living room."

I grimaced. "Holy cow. I'm sorry, Mands."

"I think a little part of me knew it was going on. He had grown distant and was staying more nights in Rochester than he was at home. I tried to make myself believe he was ministering to the homeless, but I couldn't. He told me he couldn't handle being married to me anymore. He said his job took so much out of him, and he had nothing left to give a crippled wife and two kids."

I threw my hands up. "Has he met you? I've known you for five years and had no idea you didn't have feet!"

She closed her eyes and rested her arm over her forehead. "He was making excuses for why he broke our wedding vows. Two weeks ago, he called to tell me he was getting married and wanted the kids to be part of the day."

I did the math in my head and knew it was the day I saw her sitting at the piano crying. I picked her hand up and held it in mine, rubbing the top gently.

"And that's why you've been crying? Because he's getting married again?"

"I guess," she paused and then shook her head. "No, it was more about all the pain and anguish he caused all those years ago. It dredged those feelings up again from when we divorced. He's getting married again, which means he doesn't have a problem with marriage. He simply didn't want to be married to me. I thought I was doing everything right, and giving him everything he wanted, but in the end, I couldn't give him what he needed. I wasn't enough for him."

She was crying softly again and I wiped away a tear before it ran down into her ear. "Mandy, don't you see? It's not that you weren't enough. It's that he wasn't enough. There was something inside him that made him feel like he couldn't commit to you completely. Maybe Jacob's new wife will be okay with that level of commitment, but I know you would have needed more eventually. None of this was your fault."

"I know that now, but it doesn't make it any easier to see him move on with his life as though he has no responsibilities. He wants his kids when it's convenient for him, but when it's not, he calls and cancels. Ben never wants to go there anymore. Esther usually comes home with some strange story about something that her almost new stepmommy Tasha did. I don't begrudge Jacob's happiness, but I don't want our kids to suffer because of it."

I moved off the chair and sat on the bed, pulling her up and into my arms. "I think there's been enough talk tonight. You need to rest now and let that leg heal."

I was more than a little surprised when she didn't fight against the hug. She leaned into it and rested her head on my chest. The woman was starving for attention from anyone who understood how she was feeling. She was starving for acceptance that being herself was enough. She was desperate for love on a deeper emotional plane.

I realized as she held me tightly that if she didn't get it soon, the last piece of her soul that survived his betrayal would die. I made a pact as I felt her relax into me, her body warm against mine, that I would never let that happen.

Chapter Six

I leaned into the mirror and wiped my face with the towel. After spending Friday night sleeping at Mandy's on the couch, and most of the day today keeping her company, I finally left her house for my own. I needed to shave and shower, but more than that, I needed to put some distance between us.

I ran my fingers through my damp curly hair and shook the water out a little more. I turned my head to the side and then to the other, taking a hard look at myself. My brown eyes stared back at me, asking the question I didn't want to ask myself.

Why Mandy Alexander?

I left the mirror and went back to my bedroom for clean clothes. Why Mandy Alexander? That one was easy. She was the most beautiful woman I'd ever met. Her long chestnut hair captured the face of an angel with blue eyes and tiny sweet lips I wanted to kiss. I hadn't, though. I held her in my arms last night until she slipped into dreamland and then I forced myself to let her go and sleep on the couch.

I pulled on a pair of jeans and buttoned them before pulling on my socks. She was more than a little surprised to see me this morning when she got up. She was being defiant about her wheelchair, and put on her right leg then used her crutches. Why she was so stubborn was beyond me, except I suspected that was how all the Alexanders were.

She insisted on making me breakfast since I was *still here this morning*, which was a comment that was said in disbelief. I didn't let her, of course. Instead, I whipped up some eggs and toast while she sat at the table. It was surreal to be inside Mandy's space after so many years of wondering what it was like. Her home was the perfect mix of feminine beauty and utilitarian simplicity.

It was a three-bedroom ranch with everything on one floor. It was obvious now why she lived there after the divorce. She needed the handicapped accessibility that you couldn't find in most properties in Snowberry. She had taken the small space and made it cozy and happy. The piano in the living room was the only thing that defied her neatnik persona. It was piled high with music books, sheet music, and folders.

I didn't find it messy, just the opposite was true. It felt like the only part of the house that genuinely represented the woman who lived there. She loved music, and she loved her job, two things I already knew, but it felt strangely intimate to sit on the piano bench where she spent so many hours. Even more so than sitting on her bed. The piano was where she bared her soul, not the bed.

I pulled my shirt down over my head and turned off the light in my room. I promised to be back in an hour to grill steaks for dinner. She sputtered about it, but finally relented when I told her it was steaks or I was taking her out for dinner. Since she didn't want anyone to see her without her leg, I knew exactly which one she would choose.

I opened the fridge and began pulling out meat, veggies, and barbecue sauce. It might be the beginning of October, but it wasn't too cold to grill kabobs yet. It didn't take ten minutes and I had four kabobs on a plate then I made my way back down my driveway to her house. I raised my hand to knock but heard music coming from inside. I lowered my hand and listened. She was playing *The Wind Beneath My Wings* in a way I had never heard before. It was hauntingly beautiful and I instantly knew how she got through the difficult hours of her life.

I didn't knock, but turned the knob on the door, knowing it would open. I closed it quietly and set the plate of meat on the entryway table. Leaning against the doorjamb, I watched her caress the keys as though they were the face of her lover. When she got to the song's chorus, she sang along softly. I knew she had a beautiful voice. I've heard her sing at concerts and with the kids at school dozens of times, but this was different. This was pure. It showed the depth of her voice when she was playing something that filled her emotionally. It also told me she was crazy talented in ways that went beyond teaching.

"Do you always walk into a woman's house without knocking?" she asked as she finished the last few notes.

I chuckled. "Apparently, you really do have eyes in the back of your head."

"Already told you that. Are you a slow learner?"

I picked up the meat and carried it past her toward the kitchen. "Nope, I held four degrees all before the age of thirty. I got this."

Her fingers fell off the keys in a mash of sound. "Four degrees?" she called as I tucked the meat in the fridge.

I went back to the living room and sat on the couch. "I was an overachiever."

"You don't say?" she quipped as she crutched over to the couch and settled in. I noticed she was wearing pants that were extra long for good measure. "What are the degrees in?"

"German studies and a teaching degree in German language, K-12 administration, and math education."

She cocked her head and then glanced towards the kitchen, "Wow, suddenly, I feel incredibly inferior."

"Don't, please. I mean, the first two were no brainers since I lived in Germany all my life, and the last two were ways to make a living."

She laughed and shook her head. "If you say so. I never really thought about it, but I guess you must speak German fluently."

"*Ja, und ich denke, sie sind atemberaubend.*" I smiled as though I had just told all kinds of state secrets.

She crossed her arms over her very sweet breasts. "What did you just say?"

"I said, yes, and I think you are stunning. But you weren't supposed to know that."

She blushed and I pointed at the piano, "You have a beautiful voice. I wish we got to hear it more at concerts."

"The parents are there to hear their kids, not me. I only sing if someone wants to do a duet or if they need backup. Do you sing?"

I held my hands up and laughed. "I told you before I can't carry a tune. My mom and dad made me learn how to play the guitar, though I probably couldn't play a regular one."

She stared at me, confused. "A regular one? You mean an acoustic guitar? I suppose you're one of those heavy metal guitar players."

"Oh, you would be wrong. Have you ever heard of a Schrammel guitar?" I asked.

"No kidding? You play the contraguitar?"

I held up a finger. "Played. Not so sure I could pull it off now. I think my sister still has my old one up in her attic."

"Anyone can play the guitar, Nick. Not just anyone can play the contraguitar. I bet if you picked up a six-string, you could still play it just fine. I'm a little jealous right now. I would love to be able to play a unique instrument."

I chuckled and shook my head at her. "I have it on good authority that you play plenty of unique instruments like the bassoon, mandolin, and harp."

She was about to open her mouth when there was a knock on the door. She turned her head and frowned. "I wonder who that is. I'm not expecting anyone."

She struggled to get up and I stood, motioning for her to sit with my hand. I went to the door and pulled it open. The woman on the doorstep stared up at me in surprise.

"Hello, Mrs. Alexander," I greeted her. "It's been a while since I've seen you. How are you?"

"I'm fine, Nick. I wasn't expecting you to be here," she answered and I stepped aside, so she could come through.

"I came over to make dinner for Mandy. I thought a nice steak might lift her spirits."

She held up a casserole dish and grinned. "Great minds think alike. I'll just stow this in the fridge and she can make it tomorrow night when the kids are home then."

I relieved her of the dish and motioned her in front of me. "I'll do that, you go say hi to Mandy."

I passed through the living room and held up the dish to Mands. She nodded as her mom came in. I gave them a few moments of time alone together by getting the rest of dinner ready for tonight. I lit the gas grill and let it start to heat for the kabobs then dallied in the night air. By the time I wandered back to the living room, Mandy and her mother were embracing, and I was speechless to see Suzie Alexander crying.

"Is everything all right?" I asked, putting a steadying hand on Mandy's back as she stood on crutches.

Suzie pulled back and patted her daughter's face, then wiped away her own tears. "I'm not going to let this go on any longer. I wanted her to know."

Mandy nodded and hugged her mom tightly again. "Please, don't do something that will cause a bigger rift, Mom. I'm fine, really, I am."

"You'll always be *fine*, Mandy, but I want you to be happy. In order for that to happen, I know things have to change. I love you, and enough is enough. I'll let you get back to dinner. I just had to check on you. I would have come sooner, but I had Adam, Sunny, and Jo-Jo for the day."

Mandy rubbed her mom's back and promised her she was okay. Suzie looked up at me and smiled the same smile her daughter wore. "Thanks for being here to help her, Nick. You're a good neighbor and friend."

She said the last word hesitantly and I noticed Mandy stiffen. "It's no problem. I'm just sorry this happened. I'll make sure she gets any time off she might need."

Suzie walked by me and patted my shoulder. "I have no doubt. I'll be in touch, but you're excused from Sunday dinner tomorrow, Mandy. Stay home and rest."

Mandy smiled. "Okay, bye, Mom. Thanks for dinner."

Suzie let herself out and Mandy looked exhausted from whatever their exchange had been.

"I have the grill going and I'm about to put the kabobs on. How about if I help you outside and you can enjoy the sunset while I grill?"

"Sure, that sounds nice," she said, but it was forced. I helped her to the patio doors and then over the threshold until she was settled in the chaise lounge, her leg up on a pillow.

"How's it feeling today?" I asked conversationally.

"A lot better, actually. I guess the blister was the problem. It should heal up quickly now. In fact, when I changed the bandage a few hours ago, it was already closed over and new skin was forming. The Tegaderm bandage will heal it with no scar, as long as I don't walk on it for a week or so. Once it's healed, I'll go down to Rochester and have my prosthetist cast me for new sockets. It shouldn't take long and I'll be back in business."

"Can you wear the one you have now while you wait?"

"For a few weeks, sure. They will make some modifications to make it fit better, but I may still have to use a crutch until the new ones are ready.

That's okay, it will make my whole *I hurt my ankle* story more believable to the kids."

I lowered the grill after putting the kabobs on and sat down next to her. "Have you thought about just telling them the truth?"

"Why? Do you think it would be a teachable moment, Principal Klaus? Should I tell them that I was stupid and let a drunk guy run over me while I was underage at a party? I'm sure that won't undermine my authority at all."

"Why the hostility, Mands? I simply meant telling them that you're an amputee, not how it happened. They're elementary kids, you could tell them you had an accident and that would be enough for them. Whatever, it's your choice. I'll support you no matter what you choose to do."

I stood and flipped the kabobs, dallying longer than need be to force my frustrations to simmer down. When I turned around, she was struggling to get her crutches and get up. "Mandy?"

She shook her head and didn't make eye contact with me, her crutches bumping over the threshold and away to the inside of the house. I turned the grill off and left the kabobs, then followed her into the house, and down the short hallway to her room. She was on the bed in tears again.

"Mandy, what on earth is going on? You've been in tears too many times in the last twenty-four hours for this to be just about the blister."

"Just go home, Nick. My life is falling apart and I sure as hell don't need an audience."

I sat and put my arm around her, hugging her to my side. She was stiff as a board and not interested in being comforted. "The blister is just a minor setback, love. You have to have dealt with these things many times over the last fifteen years, no?"

"It's not the blister, Nick. My mom is going to ruin everything and I couldn't convince her not to." Her voice was low and hoarse but filled with pain.

I rocked her gently in my arms and tried to figure out what she was talking about. "Is that what your mom was talking about when I came in earlier?"

"She's going to have it out with my father tonight and then call a family meeting after Sunday dinner tomorrow."

"What is she going to have out with your father? I'm confused."

"There's a reason my dad wouldn't come over here last night to help me."

"I just thought it was because he's an obstetrician and not a wound specialist."

"He is an obstetrician, but he could have easily looked at the wound and taken care of it for me. He just didn't want to. He's practicing tough love."

"He's practicing tough love on a thirty-four-year-old single mother of two doing her best to support herself and her kids? That's not tough love, that's being an ass, pardon my language."

She shrugged and sat up, wiping her face. "It's

been this way since I left the hospital all those years ago. We don't talk about Mandy's legs, and we don't talk about how she embarrassed us. We don't talk about Jacob cheating on her, because it was surely her fault, and we don't talk about any struggles she might be going through because the reason she's struggling is due to her bad choices."

I let out the breath I was holding. "That doesn't sound like the Tom and Suzie I know. They have always been so supportive of Jay, and now with Adam living with Dully and Snow."

"I guess appearances can be deceiving, at least what you see from the outside looking in. Listen, I love my parents and they're wonderful to my kids. I know if push comes to shove and I really needed something, or my kids did, my family wouldn't hesitate to make sure it happened. But I know the heavy dose of guilt that would come with it, isn't worth it. My mom has always helped as much as she can, without my dad knowing. He made sure I got good care and good legs. He made sure I went to college and could make a living. He said the rest is up to me now. I chose to marry Jacob and have kids with him."

"Okay, but you didn't choose for him to cheat on you, while as a pastor, no less."

"He thinks I should have known Jacob had moral problems because of the accident. Here's the thing, we all make mistakes when we're young. Apparently, he never did and he's perfect."

I hugged her and kissed the top of her head,

trying to think of something to say to comfort her. "I'm sorry, Mandy. You don't deserve to be treated that way. I understand what he wanted to teach you, but now he's taken it too far. None of this is your fault. Why, all of a sudden, is your mom putting her foot down?"

"I guess last night he said he was teaching me a lesson by not coming to help me. Making me go to the ER and pay a co-pay would teach me more than him coming to *rescue* me."

"Wow," I said, leaving it at that. I knew it would be better if I didn't say what I was really thinking.

"I'm glad that Jay sent December, but I feel bad for putting her in the middle of it, too."

"But at least she came and helped. He thinks that making you pay for a co-pay to the ER is going to teach you a lesson, but he doesn't understand that the only thing you're learning is that you will have to keep wearing the legs that don't fit. If you spend two hundred dollars at the ER, that's money you could have put toward new legs, if only he had come and helped!" I ran my hand through my hair and she laid her hand on my arm to calm me.

"He hasn't quite grasped that Jacob is never going to pay for them, Nick. My father holds people to a much higher standard than most people can obtain."

"I'm starting to see that."

She shook her head. "I'm not being fair. My dad is a good, hard-working, honest man. He expected a lot from us kids, because he gave us everything we could ever want, or need, in life to be successful. As the oldest child, of course, I was going to be the first to screw up. I just didn't plan on screwing up this bad." She waved at her feet and frowned. "Needless to say, my brothers learned from my mistakes and never did anything as stupid." She fell silent and laid her head on my shoulder.

"Honey, please stop saying you're stupid. It bothers me in so many ways. We all make mistakes."

She shrugged. "I've made more than my fair share, I guess. Mom also told me that dad is mad about Jacob getting married again. He's irritated that he can afford a wedding, but barely pays his child support, and it's usually late."

"I suppose any dad would think that way, love. Doesn't mean it's true," I said.

"Jacob is having a small wedding at his church with a backyard barbeque for family, that's all. It's not going to be a big wedding. Hell, ours wasn't a big wedding. We couldn't afford it after the accident, and no one else was paying for it. We got married in Rochester at his church with just our families there. It didn't matter to me. The wedding wasn't why I was getting married."

"As it should be," I agreed.

She raised one brow at me. "Have you ever been married, Nick?"

"No, I've never been married. I lived with a woman for ten years, but never quite committed. What does that tell you?"

"That you didn't love her?"

"No, I loved her, just not in the right way. I think if we had gotten married, it would have been about the wedding, and not what came after. We parted ways and though I was sad, it was more like I had lost a friend rather than a life partner."

"At least you were smart enough to figure it out before you got married and had kids."

I shrugged. "Don't second guess why you married Jacob. Look at those two beautiful kids you have. Can you imagine life without them?"

She smiled for the first time since Suzie left. "I really can't. I love them so much and they're the reason I do what I do day in and day out. They are the reason I didn't get new legs this summer. I wanted them to go to camp, and that ate up the extra cash I had to put toward the co-pays. I thought I could make it through until my tax return came in. Being an amputee for so many years, I usually have a long, slow descent into needing new legs."

"You're a wonderful mom, Mandy. You have to take care of yourself to stay that way, though."

"I know. Like I said, I really shouldn't need new ones already."

"So, why do you?"

"I guess because I've lost weight. It's possible my legs have atrophied enough to make this set of legs too big, so I slop around in them. Whatever the reason, I just have to do it."

"Can they make that pair smaller?"

She gave me the so-so hand. "They can add padding to take up space on the inside, but they will have to be remade. The padding might buy me a few months, but it could cause more blisters. I have enough to pay for one, and I'll work out a payment plan with them on the other. They're usually pretty good about that."

I held her and let her rest while I processed what she told me. I would do whatever I had to in order to get her new legs, even if I had to stick my nose in where it didn't belong.

"Nick, I know I haven't been the nicest person to you. I want you to know that it wasn't you," she said, and I chuckled.

"The old saying *it wasn't you, it was me*, right?"

She nodded. "It was me. I don't date and it takes me a long time to trust a man."

"Is five years long enough?" I asked, gazing down into her tired face.

"It appears it is," she whispered, reaching up and running her hand through my curls. "I've wanted to do that for years."

I took her hand down and held it in mine, then lowered my lips to hers. Our lips touched and I bit back the moan that almost escaped. She let a soft sigh escape and I had to clamp down hard on my self-control to keep from taking her right there on the bed. Only her words kept me grounded. She trusted me now, and I had to nurture that if I ever wanted more than a stolen kiss in the night.

I pulled my lips from hers and ran my thumb

along her bottom lip. "And I've wanted to do that for years."

She put her arms around my neck and held me, her chin resting over my shoulder. "What's happening to us, Nick?"

I turned my head and kissed her temple, the smell of her perfume enveloping me. "I don't know, but right now, I like the way this feels. Maybe we should just enjoy it and see what happens?"

She didn't answer, just held onto me a little tighter in the silence of the room.

Chapter Seven

I loosened my tie and poured a scotch over rocks, sipping it while I shrugged out of my suit coat and pulled the tie over my head. I hated wearing a suit and tie to school, but today I wasn't dealing with second graders who couldn't get along. I was interviewing possible candidates for the fourth-grade position that opened up when Mrs. Hunt had to retire unexpectedly. We ended up having to hire a long-term sub since our pool of candidates was limited. Hopefully, in the spring, there will be qualified applicants available.

I sat with the district administrator for a long while after the interviews hashing out ways to find more qualified teachers for the district, and then to devise ways to keep them. It was an undertaking that was daunting but necessary. If we could slow the turnover rate of teachers the district currently holds, we might be able to offer more advanced classes and get fresh, well-trained staff to teach them.

I set my drink down on the nightstand and changed into a pair of sweatpants and a t-shirt. I had some yard work to do and I needed to stretch out after such a long day of sitting. I didn't see Mandy today, so I wasn't able to check on her like I had the past two days. I hadn't been back to the house since I left Sunday night, either.

December brought Ben and Esther home, and after taking a look at the blister, she had declared Mandy able to return to work on her crutches. Thankfully, Mandy didn't put up a fight and agreed to the stipulations. I snuck out when Esther and Ben were busy telling their mom about their weekend. I was intruding on them at that point and they needed some family time to finish the weekend. I had been there long enough, and if I didn't separate myself from her, I wasn't sure I would be able to.

Saturday night, after our kiss, we finished our kabobs and enjoyed dinner on the patio, talking about school, music, and Germany. She surprised me with how much she knew about the country and the culture. She begged me to teach her a curse word in German, so she could use it when she didn't want anyone to know she was cursing. I had laughed for five minutes straight about that. As soon as I got myself under control, the image of her yelling a German curse word went through my mind and I started laughing all over again. To make her happy, I taught her how to say moron and promised her another lesson soon. I stole a few more kisses from her before she went to bed in her own room, and I came home to mine. She insisted I didn't need to sleep there, and I knew she was right, even though I wanted to.

I was back bright and early to check on her, though. After breakfast from Kiss's Café, she treated me to a lovely concert of songs she was planning for the holiday concert. It seemed a little early for Christmas music, but I knew she didn't have that many instructional days left before the concert season started.

I sipped coffee and listened to her soft soprano voice singing some of my favorite elementary carols. She moved on and played some of the songs for the fall concert she would do at the high school and that was the music that brought her to life. It was mesmerizing to watch her hands move across the keyboard, but when she sang, it went straight to my heart. I'm almost thirty-six-years-old and I've never felt the way I felt on Sunday. It told me a lot about the things she kept hidden from the rest of the world. I could have listened to her all day if December hadn't shown up with the kids.

I shook my head and grabbed the rake off the side of the garage. It was time to get all the final leaf stragglers into a pile to bag. It was October now and most of my trees had already shed their leaves, but the few stubborn ones were floating lazily to the ground a couple at a time. It seemed early, but I was happy to get this job done before the snow came, unlike some years.

"Hi, Nick," Ben said as he came through the trees.

I leaned on my rake. "Hi, Ben, what's happening? Is your mom okay?"

He tucked his basketball under his arm. "Yeah, she's helping Esther with her homework. Can I talk to you for a minute?"

I noticed the boy's expression was serious, so I nodded and leaned the rake back against the wall. "Why don't we sit? I'm thirsty. Do you want a root beer?"

"Sure, that would be great." He plopped down in the lawn chair in much the same way kids do when they are forced into my office; slouched, arms crossed, and legs swinging.

I pulled two root beers from the fridge and carried them back to the patio, handing him one. "What's on your mind?"

"I just wanted to say thank you for helping my mom this weekend. I wasn't here and I know my grandpa wouldn't help her. He's a jerk to her sometimes."

"Ben," I said, but he glared up at me fiercely.

"Look, forget it, thanks for taking care of Mom," he got up, but I reached out and took his arm.

"I want to hear what you have to say, Ben. Please, sit." I motioned and he glanced at the chair and back to the house a couple times, but finally chose to sit.

"He doesn't treat her the same way he treats my uncles. He acts like everything is her fault, and it's not. So, anyway, I appreciate that you were able to convince Aunt December to come and fix her leg."

I eyed the boy and decided to go with honesty. "I didn't convince her. Jay sent her after he heard your grandpa had refused to come. December was very good to your mom and made sure she was going to be okay before she left."

"That's good. My Uncle Jay knows my mom wouldn't go to the ER if she were hurt, because he's the same way. He's in a wheelchair, you know."

I nodded. "Yeah, I know. It seems like your family has had its fair share of hardships."

He shrugged. "It's just our family, that's what makes me so mad about Grandpa Tom. He treats Jay like a crystal vase and my mom like she's invincible. She's not invincible, even if she thinks she is. She spends so much time trying to prove to him she's not the same person she was as a kid. Even Esther and I have noticed."

"What do you want to happen, Ben?"

He shrugged again. "I guess I just want everyone to be treated equally like you should be in a family. My mom works hard and she doesn't ask anyone to help her with anything. I got really angry when I found out that he wouldn't help her."

I leaned in on my elbows and twisted the can in my hand. "From what I hear, you weren't the only one."

He gazed expectantly at me and I leaned in closer. "You didn't hear this from me, but your Grandma Suzie came by on Saturday and she was going to put her foot down with your grandpa this weekend."

He lowered his soda can from his mouth, "Whoa, I didn't see that coming. What happened?"

I leaned back in the chair. "I don't know. I haven't had a chance to talk to your mom about it, but maybe you should ask her. Maybe you should tell her how you feel, so she can explain things to you a little bit better."

"You said shoulda, woulda and coulda are useless words."

I laughed and nodded. "I did say that, and they are, but should and shoulda are two different tenses, right?"

He nodded, tapping on his can. "Should is present tense and shoulda is past tense, even though it's not a real word."

"Right, so should means you haven't done what you should not do, yet, and shoulda means you did what you shouldn't have and now you wish you hadn't. Am I making myself clear?"

"Yes, sir, I mean, Nick." He nodded and drank from his can, watching the birds fly around the feeder.

"Is that what you wanted to talk about?" I asked, convinced it wasn't.

"Did you know that Mom was an amputee?" he asked, his head turned to the side.

"No, I had no idea. Looking back, I guess I see it now, but not having any indication there was a problem, I just thought that was how she walked. Other than a slight sway, she walks like you and I do."

"Did it bother you?" he asked. I could tell he was going for nonchalant, even if I could read him like a book.

"Did what bother me?"

He motioned at his legs. "You know."

"Did it bother me that she doesn't have feet, or did it bother me to see her without feet?"

"Either," he answered immediately, and then just as quickly changed his mind, "or both."

I shook my head. "No, I'm not bothered knowing that she doesn't have feet. It also didn't bother me when she wasn't wearing her legs. What it showed me was how strong she must be to go about her daily life, teach, and raise you and Esther alone. Do you think it should bother me?"

"No, it's just, I know it bothered my dad and that's why I asked." He drank from his pop can and pretended I wasn't there as he thought about whatever was really bothering him. "Ben, is something going on you don't want to talk to your mom about?"

He refused to look at me, but he answered after a few moments. "I was just wondering if you thought I had to go to my dad's wedding."

"Well, Ben, it really doesn't matter what I think. That's between you, your dad, and your mom."

"He really wants us to come."

"You're his kids. I'm sure he wants you there to celebrate that day with him."

"What if I don't want to celebrate that day with him?"

This was dangerous territory. On the one hand, he needed someone to talk to, and on the other hand, I had to be very careful about what I said. Going or not going to his father's wedding was something that wasn't my decision to make. I switched into principal mode to sort it out. "Can you tell me why you wouldn't want to celebrate with him?"

He turned to me then, and his face was beet red with eyes of fire. It reminded me a lot of when his mom got mad, and I tried not to smile. "Do you know what he did to our family?" he asked, his tone filled with anger and hurt. I nodded without speaking. "Would you want to go to his wedding and pretend to be happy about it?" I shook my head no. "Me, either." He sank back into the chair and kicked his legs some more, anger still radiating from him.

"What part about him getting remarried is really bothering you, Benji?"

"Would you please not call me that? I prefer Ben."

"Of course, I'm sorry, Ben it is."

"Have you ever walked in on your dad naked with another woman before, Nick?"

I was taking a drink of root beer and nearly choked when I tried to swallow. I coughed a few times and finally held my hand up. "No, I can't say that I have. My father is dead."

"Oh, I'm sorry," he answered, staring down at the ground.

"It was a long time ago, Ben. What happened between your parents was a long time ago, too, but it appears it still upsets you. You were very young when your parents broke up. How much do you really remember?"

"I was five and I will never forget what I saw that day, Nick, ever. Maybe at five I didn't know why he was standing there naked with another woman who wasn't my mom, but I understand it all very well now."

"I suppose you do," I said, trying not to be judgmental toward his father. I had to stay neutral. I had to be Switzerland.

"Does it make me a bad person for not loving him very much?"

"Whoa, Ben, I think maybe you need to talk with your mom about this. I will go with you if you want."

"That means you do think that makes me a bad person."

"I didn't say that, but if you're that upset about your dad, then maybe you need to talk to someone to work through it."

"I'm talking to you," he said as though I didn't have four degrees.

"Okay, then I'll answer. I don't think it makes you a bad person. I think it makes you a hurt, angry, and sad person, at least when it comes to your relationship with your dad. My guess is you don't trust him very much?"

"I don't trust him at all, and I don't understand why Tasha does either. He slept around on my mom, so what makes her think he won't sleep around on her?"

I blew out a breath. "You're asking very adult-like questions here, Ben. Where are you hearing this? Your mom, your grandpa, or your uncles?"

He crossed his arms over his chest. "I have a brain, Nick. It doesn't take more than first-grade math to add one and one and get two. My dad is very …" he snapped his fingers, clearly looking for a word. "You know he says one thing but does the other."

"Hypocritical."

His fingers snapped once and he pointed at me. "Yes! He's hypocritical. He's a minister, right?" he asked and I nodded. "Well, he stands up in front of people every Sunday and tells them not to sin, and to follow the Ten Commandments, but then he does the exact opposite. How is that cool?"

I took a drink to keep from laughing aloud at his verbiage. "It's not cool, not at all. You're right, he's very hypocritical. We have a saying in Germany that goes, *handlungen des Menschen werden Ihnen sagen, alles, was Sie wissen müssen*."

"Wow, you speak German?" he asked in awe.

"I was born and raised in Germany by a German father, so yes, I speak German. What I just said means *a man's actions will tell you everything you need to know*."

He sat swinging his feet for several more minutes and then stood and picked up his basketball. "Thanks for the talk, Nick. That really helped."

"It did?" I asked, confused.

"You said a man's actions will tell you everything you need to know. I could go home and tell my mom I don't want to go to Dad's wedding, and she wouldn't make me, but it would cause a big problem for her and for my sister. It would also embarrass my dad if I refused to come, and it might ruin his day. I don't have to like it, but I will go because that's the right thing to do, and that's the kind of man I want to be."

The kid absolutely nailed it. I would tell his mother what a wonderful son she was raising at some point, but first, I raised my fist and he gave it a bump.

"Excellent work, son. I'm proud of you, and your mom will be, too."

"Thanks, Nick, but we all have to do things in life we don't want to do. Look at my mom, she does all kinds of things she doesn't want to do and doesn't complain about it. I shouldn't either." He walked to the end of the driveway and turned back to face me. "Hey, Nick?"

I stood and walked up the driveway a bit, "Yeah, Ben?"

"What does the S stand for in your name?"

I laughed and shook my head. "I can't tell you that. It's too embarrassing."

"If I were to guess it, would you tell me if I was right?"

"If you managed to guess this name, then yes, I would tell you, but you'll never guess."

"Give me time and I just might." He started walking backward away from me. "Mom said you two are taking us to the fire hose competition on Saturday for Fall Fest. Is that true?"

"We did talk about doing that before she hurt her leg, but if she's okay to go, then I'll happily tag along."

He didn't hide the fist pump he gave as he walked away.

Chapter Eight

"Saxon?" Ben asked and I shook my head. "Saxler?" I shook my head no again. "Schlitterbahn?"

I laughed straight away at that one. "That's a water park in Texas!"

He shrugged. "I know, but it means *slide* in German, so I thought I would give it a whirl. Besides, it's fun to say."

"I'll give you that, but why all the German names?"

"You're a junior, right?" he asked and I nodded. "You told me that your dad was German, and if you're a junior, then that means you're named after your dad who would be named something German and not English. I think anyway."

"That's excellent deduction, my boy, but you still haven't guessed it."

"Oh, nuts," he frowned, but it quickly turned into a smile when he turned to watch the fire hose competition again.

"This place is nuts," I laughed, watching the firemen shaking hands with each other.

Mandy wore a big smile on her face and

was clapping loudly for the Snowberry team. Her brother, Dully, was team captain and her younger brother, Bram, was backing him up. She leaned over toward me. "We may be little in Snowberry, but we can be loud!" To make her point, she stuck her fingers between her teeth and whistled so loud I thought my ears would bleed. I was laughing, though, and so were Ben and Esther. They both jumped up when their uncles jogged over, Bram set Esther on his shoulders and Dully piggybacked Ben around the wet street, kicking water at each other with their big boots.

"Man, it's a beautiful day out today," Mandy said, watching her kids belly laugh and soak up the sun.

"I know something else that's beautiful," I said and she leaned in again.

"What's that?" she asked, her eyes still trained on her kids.

"You."

She turned her head to gaze at me and patted my face. "Teacher's pet."

"That would be okay," I whispered into her ear, sitting behind her in the bleachers. She looked up at me and laughed a little self-consciously. I had to bite the inside of my lip hard to keep from leaning down to kiss her. Ben and Esther ran back to us at that moment and were jumping around.

"Mom, Uncle Dully and Uncle Bram are taking Adam and Sunny to the rubber duck races; can we go?"

Dully waved at his sister to let her know to send the kids, so she agreed. "Tell Uncle Dully we will work our way down there when the crowd thins, okay?"

"Okay, Mom," Ben said, ready to run, but I grabbed his arm.

I dug in my pocket and handed the kids ten bucks each. "Get yourself something to eat or put some cash down on the ducks, your choice."

"Thanks, Nick!" they both said in unison and tore off toward Dully.

I sat next to her now that the kids were gone and she turned to stare at me, her eyebrows up, and her hair flying around her face. "Did you just tell my children to play the ponies?"

"Essentially, but you know the money goes to a good cause, so in this case, it's totally acceptable to condone gambling."

"Ah, yes, the Snowberry Coats for Kids can usually buy a dozen coats with the money from all that gambling. Are you going to be part of the program again this Christmas?"

I stared at her, taken aback. "Have you heard something I haven't? Tell me they haven't replaced me with a different jolly old St. Nick."

She laughed and pushed me in the shoulder gently. "You're hilarious." She stuck her tongue out at me for a second then pulled it back in before anyone saw. "I haven't heard of any new St. Nicks showing up around these parts."

"Well, that's mighty fine then, little lady, 'cause

these parts got all the St. Nicks they need," I drawled in quite possibly, the worst western accent ever.

She groaned and shook her head, but was laughing when she did it. She pointed toward the lake. "Should we work our way over to the lake and see what kind of trouble the kids are getting into?"

"Sure, would you like to drive over to the boat landing where they are setting the ducks free?"

She turned and her eyes flared, just like her son's. "I'm not crippled, Nick. I can walk."

I took her shoulders and peeked out at her from under my curls. "I didn't say you were crippled, but it's a long way there. I noticed you're walking much better and without your crutches. I didn't want you to feel like you had to walk if you would rather rest the leg some more. That's all."

She refused to make eye contact for a long time and when she did, I knew she felt terrible, which was not what I wanted either. "I'm defensive about my feet because they've made me defensive."

"Who are they?"

"My dad and Jacob," she answered, staring over my shoulder at the lake beyond.

"Have I ever made you feel like you need to be defensive about your feet?" She shook her head and I rubbed her forearms when a cool wind blew across us. "Then how about from now on, anytime I ask you something about your legs, you know that I'm simply asking to give you a choice, not to make you look weak, or to make you feel like you need to prove something to me, okay?"

She nodded and gave me a soft, *okay,* before standing. I helped her down from the bleachers, where she hesitated on the ground.

"I want to walk because it's a nice day today, but we have the Minnesota Educators Association Conference in a few days …" she paused when a loud cheer went up from the lakeside.

"And MEA will require lots of standing and walking on already tired legs?"

"Yeah, I guess maybe we could drive down there and then walk along the lakeshore and watch the ducks make their way across the lake. Maybe we'll even find my children and their bookies on the way."

That moment when her words made sense in my mind was lost by the way the sun shone on her face. I lost all semblance of intelligence and leaned in, kissing her right there in the middle of the town square. Her hands grabbed my jacket, but instead of pushing me away, she pulled me closer. I didn't let the kiss linger, but ended it after just enough of our hunger was satisfied to get us through until the next time we were alone.

I turned and took her hand in mine, walking toward the corner where I had parked her small wagon. "I think that's a great idea."

I unlocked the door and helped her in, then went to the driver's side and put the car in gear, steering it down the small road used for boats in the summer.

"Did your mom call you after she talked to your dad?"

She shook her head. "I saw her the other day. He wasn't overly receptive, from what I understand. He told her she was being a drama queen and then forbade her from bringing it up at dinner on Sunday. She didn't, but she said he has been very quiet and hanging out in the woodshop when he's not at work, which means he's thinking."

"Or angry?" I asked, but she shook her head.

"No, when he hangs out in the woodshop and does nothing but carve and sand, he's thinking."

"Maybe that's an okay thing. If he's taking time to think about what's happened, and how he treats you, then he knows what your mom said holds merit."

"Is it wrong of me to hope that's true?"

"I don't think so. You've been through a lot and the one man who should always be there to hold you up is your father. I hope he comes around and sees that, too."

"To be honest, I would just be happy if he cut me a little slack once in a while. I feel bad that Esther will never have a dad like that, either."

"How do you know?" I asked, parking the car alongside several others who had driven to the lake.

"You've never met Jacob, but he's not exactly Dad of the Year material."

"Ben mentioned that," I agreed, then grimaced when I realized what I said. "Ben talked to me the other day about his dad and how he was feeling about the wedding. I don't want to say anything he may have shared in confidence, but I will tell you that you have so much to be proud of in that boy. He's only eleven, but he's already three times the man his father is."

I took her hand and brought it to my lips, brushing a kiss across her knuckles. She stared ahead at the lake and the few red and orange leaves waving in the wind. "Thank you for sharing that with me. It means a lot to know I'm doing okay by him. I don't want you to break any confidences either, but is there anything I need to know? Are they not safe with Jacob?"

"He didn't say anything about not being safe. He was struggling with the kind of man his father is. We talked about it and I told him he gets to be whatever kind of man he wants to be, regardless of who his father is. He seemed to understand that straight away, but felt like it would make him a bad person for not loving Jacob the way he thinks he should."

She nodded. "He can't forgive his dad for what he did. I try so hard never to say a bad thing about him in front of the kids. It's my belief that kids shouldn't have to be weighed down with the things that happen between adults. Unfortunately, Jacob brought that home to roost when Ben was old enough to remember it."

She turned to me and picked fake lint off my sweatshirt, just to do something with her hands.

"Does he need to see a counselor? I've never offered, but if you think he does, then I'll find one and figure out a way to pay for it."

I stopped her hands before she picked all the fleece off my shirt. "I don't think he needs a counselor. I think he needs someone to do things with him and let him talk. I got the vibe that Jacob doesn't do that?"

"Nope, if he's home, then they do things as a family. Tasha has a boy and a girl, too. If he's not home, then Tasha leaves them to play among themselves. It's not ideal, but it is court-ordered. Dully and Bram include him in everything they can, and my dad plays basketball with him, but I'm not sure he would open up to any of them."

"Not the way he feels about your dad," I muttered.

"What?"

"I said that aloud, didn't I?" I asked and she nodded, her eyes wide. "He told me he thinks your dad is a jerk sometimes. Those were his words, not mine," I said, holding my hands up in defense. "It makes him angry that he treats you differently compared to the way he treats Jay. I think that was in confidence, though, so please don't mention it."

"He's said the same to me in so many words, only he left the word jerk off when he said it to me." I gave her a rueful smile and a shoulder shrug. "I know he feels comfortable with you and will say things to you he won't say to family. I'm okay with that as long as you are. If he has someone he can talk to and not feel like he has to censor his real feelings, then I think that's good for him, no?"

"I'm willing to talk to or hang out with Ben anytime he needs me, as long as you trust I will tell you if he says something that isn't safe to keep between him and me."

She trailed her finger down my face and rested her hand on my shoulder. "That's one thing I don't have to worry about. You're a mandatory reporter."

I laughed and shook my head at her words, then climbed from the car. I pulled her door open and helped her out, then put my arm around her waist and walked with her down to the lake.

"Maybe you should take your arm off me. I'm sure other people from school will be here."

"I've already seen half a dozen. I don't have a problem with it if you don't, but if you want me to, I will."

"I don't really want you to. It feels nice to be supported, physically and emotionally. I'm not too proud to admit that."

I squeezed her waist a little bit as we walked along the lakeshore in peaceful companionship, watching the multicolored rubber ducks bobbing toward the finish line. Every so often, a boat in the middle of the lake would roar its motor, stirring up the water and sending the ducks swimming off in different directions. The kids cheered and the parents groaned as they watched their hopeful winner head to the back of the pack.

"Are you going to the MEA conference this

week?" she asked suddenly, and I gazed down at her from where we had stopped to watch the race.

"Of course, I am. School is out and I have a speech to give about budgeting in a small school. There are also several roundtable discussions I want to go to about how to lure new talent into our district. I saw your name on the materials as well."

"Great minds think alike, I guess. I'm giving a presentation on how to incorporate music into schools when budgets are tight."

"And you're going to rock it," I assured her, kissing the tip of her nose, not caring who was watching.

"The kids are going to Jacob's parents' house on Tuesday night and they will be responsible for them before, during, and after the wedding. I will need to pick them up on Sunday morning. Ben and Esther have more fun when they stay with their grandparents and just visit at Jacob's house, which says a lot. I really wanted to attend MEA, though, so I swallowed my pride and asked Annette and Larry to take them."

"And I'm sure they were glad to do it."

"They always are. I just don't like to ask. Personally, I think their father should have to be a parent occasionally. Since he's getting married, I went ahead and allowed it. Ann and Larry feel bad about what happened and always try to do what they can for the kids. We have a good relationship, even if their son and I don't."

"You'll have a whole lot of free time in St. Paul

then. Is that what you're saying?"

"I'm only going for one day. The school can't afford to pay for the hotel room and neither can I, so I'll drive home after my presentation."

"Hmm," I said, unhappy with the turn of events.

"Mom! Nick! Our duck won a prize!"

We turned and two very excited kids were running toward us. She knelt down to catch Esther and I grabbed Ben around the waist, ruffling his hair. I went through the motions of being excited, but I was really thinking about a way to keep her in St. Paul with me for a few extra days.

Chapter Nine

I heard a car screech to a halt on the street as I loaded my bags in my trunk. I turned, worried there had been an accident. Instead, one very aggravated woman was marching up my driveway and I steeled myself for the inevitable blow-up.

She moved way quicker than I expected and stuck her finger in my chest. "I. Cannot. Believe. You. Did. That. For God's sake, Nick, I will pay my own way. I will pay you back every last cent if it's the last thing I do!"

I laid my finger across her lips. "Stop, please. Don't ever say that again. My father said he would take my mother to Paris if it was the last thing he did, and it was, they died in a hotel fire on their wedding anniversary."

Her anger drained away immediately and she sagged against my finger. "I'm sorry, Nick. I didn't know what happened. That's tragic."

"It was, so don't use that phrase in my presence ever again, agreed?" I asked and she nodded like a robot.

I dropped to my knees and lifted her pant legs. "They're gorgeous. Are those music notes?" I asked, gazing up at her. She had her hands on her hips and was anything but happy. She knew I was playing her, but I didn't care. She had new legs and that was all that mattered.

"I went down there to pick them up and they wouldn't take my money. They said the bill had already been paid. I told them I wanted to know by whom and they told me it was you!"

"They weren't supposed to tell you, but I gave that a fifty-fifty chance since they're scared of you."

"They aren't scared of me, but you should be."

I laughed and shook my head. "I'm not scared of you, but they are. They didn't even want to take my money until they talked to you, but I managed to convince them. Glad I did, too, these are so pretty. They aren't made out of the same material as your old ones, are they? Are they more comfortable?"

"It's a new material that they can mold better to the bony changes of my legs, so I can go longer between sets. They can heat them up and make room if one part begins to pinch like what caused the blister last time. Yes, they are music notes, and they feel like heaven, but I'm still mad at you!"

I stood and brushed off my knees. "I can deal with that. You're standing here in beautiful new legs that are comfortable, so a few evil glares are worth it to know you aren't hurting."

She fisted one hand and pounded it on her hip. "Are you a teacher or something? You always know the right thing to say."

"Comes with the territory, love." I bent and kissed her nose.

She leaned into my chest. "Thank you, Nick. Maybe I don't understand why you paid for them, but I'm thankful that you did. I don't like being in pain, and I was every day. I don't want you to think I don't appreciate what you did."

I put my arms around her so she couldn't pull away from me. "You're welcome, Mandy. I paid for them for one reason. I don't like to see you in pain. I will do anything to make sure you aren't hurting, and that starts with a new pair of legs."

She leaned back and I reached behind me to close the trunk of my sensible American made sedan. It was boring, but it got the job done. "Now, go get your bags so we can get on the road. Reception is at six and we need to check into the hotel beforehand."

"I told you, Nick. I'm not staying at the hotel. I'll be there tomorrow in time for my presentation."

I slung my arm around her shoulder and walked with her back to her car. I stuck her in the passenger side and climbed in the driver's side, pulling it into the garage. I handed her a purse, keys, sunglasses, and a cell phone. By the time I got out of the car, she was waiting for me and I marched her right up her front walk. She unlocked the front door and I motioned her in, then closed it behind me. I deposited myself on the couch and crossed my ankles while I motioned toward her room.

"I have a suite, which is just ridiculous since it's only me, so I called the hotel and added your name to the room. Two birds, one stone."

She started shaking her finger back and forth at me. "I'm not staying in a hotel suite with you at an educator's convention, Nick. How would that look?"

I rubbed my nails on my pants a few times and then blew on them, rubbing them off again. It was driving her crazy, which was kind of fun. "I suppose it would look like two colleagues saving the school district money since that's what it is."

She threw her arms out to the side. "That would only work if we were the same sex!"

I raised one side of my lip. "What fun is that?"

"Nick!" she yelled, spinning on her heel and stomping down to her room. I could hear her throwing things around, muttering under her breath, and slamming closet doors while I played on my phone. We had plenty of time before we had to be there, which is why I didn't tell her ahead of time. It was easier this way, though the ride to St. Paul might be hell to pay.

To her credit, less than fifteen minutes later, she stood in front of me with a packed suitcase. She flopped it down on the floor next to me and began to stuff things she had taken off the piano into a smaller tote. When she was finished with that, she went about the house locking doors and windows, feeding the goldfish, and closing the curtains.

"Ready?" I asked congenially.

She grabbed the tote and went to the door, throwing it open and waiting for me to pull the suitcase over the stoop. She locked it behind us and walked ten steps ahead of me to my driveway. I clicked the trunk open and she tossed in her tote, taking her purse and slamming the car door, barely getting her foot in before it slammed.

I settled the suitcase in the trunk and shook my head. This was gonna be a long drive.

"I love the way you look sitting in my Malibu, kind of like Malibu Barbie." I grinned at the woman next to me and she rolled her eyes.

"Cute, but not."

"So, that's not cute then?" I asked, and she stuck her tongue out at me, but at least she cracked a smile. The last hour had been spent in painful silence punctuated only by her occasional grunt as she switched positions or folded her arms over her chest. The closer we got to St. Paul, the more she relaxed. Maybe she was resigning herself to the inevitable, but whatever the reason, at least she wasn't radiating anger any longer.

"Do you want to stop and get something to eat?

The reception is only drinks and hors d'oeuvres."

She checked the clock. "I suppose it is almost two and I skipped lunch."

"I know the perfect place," I promised, steering the car toward the only place that felt like home. I parked and she climbed out, reading the sign on the building in front of us. "The Glockenspiel?"

I pulled the heavy wood door open and ushered her in. "Best German food in the city. I might argue the whole state of Minnesota."

"I've never eaten German food before," she said, her nose curling up.

"Take my word for it, you're going to love it."

She didn't just take my word for it, she took my hand, which surprised the heck out of me. I held hers lightly and smiled at the hostess who came to seat us.

"*Partei von zwei*," I said and her eyes rounded.

"*Du sprichst Deutsch?*"

"*Ja, nicht viele tun?*"

She laughed and motioned us to follow her, "*nicht viele, wie jung und hübsch, wie Sie.*"

I laughed and held the chair for Mandy, then took the other seat at the two-person table. She set the menus in front of us and motioned toward the bar, "*Getränke? Bier? Wein?*"

Mandy looked confused and I took her hand. "She asked if we want anything to drink. Beer or wine?"

"Since I'm spending the night with you, I need to be on my toes. How about a Diet Coke?"

I gave her a grin and then nodded to the waitress. "Two Diet Cokes."

The waitress turned back to the bar and Mandy leaned over the table and spoke in hushed tones. "What did you two just say? You were flirting, weren't you?"

Her cheeks were fire engine red and I kissed her hand. "I wasn't. She was surprised I spoke German because not many do. At least not many as young, and cute, as I am." I winked then gave her my best sly grin.

She rolled her eyes to the ceiling. "You're cute, alright," she muttered, picking up the menu. "Whoa, that's intense."

"Before you give up, look under the German and it's all translated in English," I explained, pointing it out.

"Good, if I had to depend on you to order for me, I would probably end up with wienerschnitzel."

"What's wrong with wienerschnitzel?" I asked perplexed, and she heaved a heavy sigh of frustration.

She read the menu over and finally stared up at me. "It's still intense. I don't even know what half of this stuff is."

I raised one brow. "Do you trust me to order?"

She glanced down at the menu and finally closed it, handing it to me. "You know better than I do what this stuff is."

I chuckled and motioned for the waitress.

"We'll have the schweinesteak, hold the potato salad and substitute pommes frites, and an order of schnitzel fingers."

"Both excellent choices," the waitress agreed. "Can I start you with a *vorspeisen*?"

I looked at Mandy. "Do you want an appetizer?"

"I don't suppose you have any soft pretzels? I suddenly have a hankering for one."

The waitress grinned. "Of course, we call them *bretzel mit senf*. Would you like salt or no salt?"

"Definitely salt," Mandy nodded.

"I'll put in your order," the waitress said then disappeared inside the kitchen.

"Hankering for a pretzel?" I asked, taking both of her hands in mine.

"You bring me to a place like this and expect me not to want a pretzel? I live on soft pretzels from the freezer section."

I recoiled and scrunched up my nose. "Tell me you're kidding." She shook her head no. "How on earth do you even eat those things?"

"Well, first, I put them on a pan and wet them enough so the salt will stick, and then I bake them and dip them in cheese …" she stopped talking when she saw my face.

"Do you feed them to the kids, too?"

She shook her head. "No, they find them revolting."

I shook my hand around in confusion. "You make normal food for the kids, but you don't eat it?"

"I eat dinner with them, of course, but breakfast and lunch — pretzels."

I shivered at the thought and she laughed in a way that said she was genuinely enjoying herself.

"About to be amazed then. This *bretzel mit senf* is going to blow your mind."

As if on cue, the waitress reappeared with the pretzel and several small jars filled with different flavored mustards. Mandy rubbed her hands together, raised one brow, and then attacked them.

Chapter Ten

"I'm so full," she moaned from the passenger seat, her hand over her belly.

"I know, right? What did you think of the schnitzel fingers?"

She rolled her head toward me. "I will admit they were amazing with the lemon garlic mayo. Thank you for taking me there. It was a new experience and I love new experiences."

I smiled widely, thrilled to have made her happy. "You're welcome. We're almost to the hotel and then you can rest for a few minutes before we go to the reception."

In a few more miles, I pulled the car into the hotel parking lot and turned off the engine. She glanced around and then turned to me. "The Embassy Suites? I thought we were staying at the convention."

"Love, the convention is at the St. Paul Convention Center and they don't have a hotel. Most of us are spread out among the hotels around the Center. I know for a fact none of the other teachers from the district are staying here. I did that on purpose."

She stared at me with one eye scrunched. "You purposely booked a hotel with the intent of bringing me here?"

I shook my head. "No, I changed my reservation to here when you told me you weren't staying over. Since no one else is staying here, you don't have to worry about anyone seeing us together. The River Centre is only a mile away, so you can go back and forth between programs if you want."

She leaned back on the seat and gazed up at the large brick building. "Why am I so afraid to go in there with you?"

I turned in my seat and put my hand on her shoulder. "You don't have anything to be afraid of. If you would rather, I can get you your own room."

She shook her head. "It's not even that. I don't know what it is. This is the first time I've felt like an adult in a very long time."

"Can you explain that in a different way to me?" I asked, and she motioned at the building and then between the two of us.

"This is the first time I've been in a situation where a kid isn't going to need something from me. I'm not used to that feeling, I guess."

"You've spent the last five years being a mom and forgot how to be Mandy?"

She nodded and then shrugged. "I guess that's what I'm saying. Do you think it's like riding a bike?"

I leaned across the console and held the back of her neck lightly. I wasn't forcing her to come to me, but she did, naturally and willingly. I lowered my lips to hers and laid a kiss across them, waiting to see what she would do. Her hand came up into the hair near my ear and fisted it, holding me to her. I gazed into her eyes and saw how scared she was, but there was desire in them, too.

I deepened the kiss until her lips parted and allowed me in. She tasted of sweet-spicy mustard and I moaned softly when her tongue caressed mine. Knowing that she wanted me to kiss her, to touch her, to show her how to be Mandy again, was more than I could ask for. I had waited patiently for so many years to find the right woman. Had I found her? I could feel my lower half growing in response to the way her kiss made me feel, knowing how wonderful it would feel to have her tongue stroking me in all the right places.

I slowed the pace of the kiss until our lips fell apart. Her mouth stayed open a bit and her bottom lip was plump and wet. I bit down gently on it with my teeth, sucking lightly until she whimpered. I released it after a moment and rested my forehead on hers.

"How did that feel?" I whispered, and she shuddered a little in my arms.

"Just like riding a bike."

She smiled, and I hugged her to me, content to be the one to teach her that lesson again.

I held the door with one hand, a bag in the other, so she could enter the suite. She looked beat and I noticed she was limping a little on her left leg. She sank down onto the small couch and laid her head back.

"That went way longer than I thought it would."

"No kidding," I agreed, setting the bag down on the bar that separated the living room from the small bedroom. There was a fridge, and since I stopped off at the liquor store on the way back here, now there was a nice bottle of wine. I shrugged out of my coat and hung it over the back of the chair, then came around and knelt in front of her, lifting her pant leg.

"What are you doing?" she asked, slamming her hand down over her calf.

"I'm checking your leg. I noticed you were limping and I'm worried you have another blister."

"I don't. They're just new legs and I need to break them in."

I felt a smile tugging on my lips. "Kind of like a new pair of shoes?"

She leaned her head back on the couch. "Exactly, that's the perfect comparison. Like a new pair of shoes, you have to wear them for a bit. You have to get the limbs used to the tighter fit when you've been slopping around in the other pair for so long."

I pulled the Velcro straps open and removed the plate, revealing her leg in the liner. She pulled her leg out, her shoulders slumping in resignation that I was going to check and be sure she wasn't lying. I rolled the liner down, inspecting the bones and skin, then ran my hands up and down her leg. She shuddered every time I got near the bottom of her leg.

"Am I hurting you?" I asked, trying to gauge why she was reacting so strongly to my touch.

"No, but please stop. I'm not comfortable with this."

"Because?" I asked, my hands stilling near her anklebone.

"Only one man has seen them, Nick, and he cheated on me because of it."

"He didn't cheat because of your legs, Mandy. He cheated because that's the kind of person he was."

"But if I had been more …"

"More what? More sexy?"

She shrugged. "I guess. I mean, I had two feet when we met, and now, I don't."

I ran my hands back up her leg again while I spoke softly to her. "People change, love. That's supposed to be how it works. We're supposed to grow and change, but if both people in the relationship don't change, then you'll grow apart.

Jacob was stuck in the past, wanting a relationship he used to have that was no longer there. That didn't make it your fault. You have more than made something of your life. Let me ask you something?"

She motioned toward me as if to say, *why not, you're already ruining my day*.

"Did the two of you have an active sex life?"

"What does that have to do with my legs?" she asked defensively.

"Answer the question, please."

"I never turned him down when he asked, but we only had sex when he wanted it, at least after we were married. If I asked and he didn't want to, then we didn't."

"And when you had it, was it mutually satisfying?"

She laid her arm across her forehead and eyed me from underneath it. "I'm not comfortable talking about this with you, Nick. It's ancient history, what does it matter?"

"It matters a great deal, actually. Was it mutually satisfying?"

"I can't speak for him, but he seemed happy to roll over and go to sleep."

"And for you?" She barely shook her head, but it was enough for me to know the answer. "And that's the reason you've gone so many years being alone. You think you can never keep a man happy unless your body is perfect, no?"

"There are other ways to satisfy those desires

than having a man in my bed, Nick. I have an endless supply of batteries and no headaches to deal with in the morning."

I let my hands stroke further up her leg and across her thighs, running them dangerously close to the center of her triangle. Her breath became shorter and quicker each time my hand touched her skin on the way back to her ankle.

"No toy is going to give you the same feeling of being well-loved and sexually satisfied as being in a relationship with another human being. Toys can be a fun part of that relationship, but they shouldn't replace it. Do you think Jacob simply wasn't happy, or do you think he just couldn't deal with your legs?"

She shrugged. "I think it was both. To be honest, I'm not sure if we hadn't had the accident that our relationship would have lasted to the marriage point, but like I said, that's ancient history."

"If it's ancient history, why does what he thought about your legs still matter?"

"I don't know, Nick."

"The answer is, it doesn't. He is no longer of any significance to your personal life or self-esteem. He may be your children's father, but that's the only place he belongs in your life."

"What are you trying to say?" she asked, her head cocked.

"I'm trying to say that you've got to stop punishing yourself for what happened with him and start living your life again. You exude strength in public, yet privately you stumble over the thing that makes you strong." I unfastened the second leg and slid it off, holding her legs together by the knees. "Your legs are beautiful because they're yours. They carry you everywhere you need to go and they make beautiful music. Maybe you need extra help in pushing down that pedal on the piano in public, but I can look at this leg," I held up her right leg and rubbed the skin on the bottom that was a large calloused area, "and know that in private you don't wear your leg when you play."

"You're good," she smiled and I laid her leg back down against the couch.

"It's not that I'm good. I just see the whole person. I have a hard time separating a person out into parts and parcels because each part isn't the same without the parcel."

"That doesn't even make sense, Nick."

"Yes, it does. You aren't the same person you would be if you still had two feet, so your part wouldn't be the same," I laid my hand on her chest over her heart, "if it weren't for the parcels," I explained, resting my hand on her legs.

She closed her eyes while I massaged her legs a bit longer. Finally, she put her hand over mine. "You really are right, you know. Why do you have to be right all the time?"

"It comes as a package deal with your administration degree," I teased. I lifted myself onto the couch next to her and brushed the hair from her forehead. She rolled her head toward me and smiled. "My legs don't bother you?"

I lowered my lips to hers in a slow descent that gave her enough time to see every single intention I had flare to life in my eyes. When our lips touched, she was already reaching for my hair and I was pulling her toward me onto my lap. I forced my lips to stay closed and move off hers and into the crook of her neck. She let her head fall back and I kissed every inch of her soft, tender neck.

"Your legs don't bother me in the least, but I'm not a leg man," I whispered against her neck, reaching my tongue up to swipe at her earlobe.

"What kind of man are you?" she asked, her head arching back a little further with my touch.

She was on my lap and my hand was resting on her shoulder. I dragged it lower to the soft edge of her breast, running one finger down the outside and to the rib right below it. "I'm much more about the ladies."

She snickered and then tucked her forehead against my shoulder, slowing her breathing, and stopping the trail I was making to her lips.

"I think I need a nice dip in a cold pool," I admitted, kissing her ear and moving her off my lap and back to the couch. "Do you feel up to a dip in the whirlpool downstairs?"

She worried her bottom lip between her teeth. "Whirlpools aren't cold. I think that would only add to the *hot and bothered* feeling we currently have."

"All the same, it would feel good."

"I can't wear my legs in the water and I can't get in or out of the water without my legs."

"That's easily solved. They have a chair lift here for the pool and whirlpool."

"Really?" she asked, surprised.

I nodded. "One of the reasons I chose this hotel."

"You're making the whole spontaneity thing seem much more planned out, Nick."

I shrugged. "Just being honest. You in?"

She held up her palms. "'Fraid not, I don't own a suit. I haven't gone swimming in fifteen years."

I stared at her in disbelief. "What about with the kids?"

She shook her head. "Tell me how, Nick."

"Is it safe for you to go swimming, like as far as the skin goes?"

She looked at the bottom of the leg again and shrugged. "I don't see why not. The blister is healed. I could put a waterproof cover over it to keep it free from bacteria, but I don't have a suit."

I stood and grabbed my wallet from my coat, then brought her cosmetic bag back to her from her suitcase. "Excellent, you do that and I'll go get you a suit."

I was at the door by the time she got my name out. "Nick, the closest store is miles away."

"I happened to see suits downstairs in the gift shop." I ran my finger up and down around her body a few times. "Size eight?"

She chuckled. "I've had two kids, but nice try,

Rico Suave. Try a size ten."

I grinned and she smacked herself in the forehead with her hand, knowing I won this round.

"Size ten it is. I'll be right back. Don't go anywhere."

I was out the door and it was closing as she yelled, "No bikini!"

Chapter Eleven

"Now, was that so bad?" I asked her as we settled into the hot tub. It was nearly nine, but she was next to me and that's all I cared about.

"You did okay with the suit," she admitted glancing down at her chest. "It might be a little tight here." She motioned at her chest and I lifted one side of my lips in a salute.

"And that's just the way I like it."

She laid her head back on the edge of the tile and laughed, "You're a male chauvinist at heart, aren't you?"

"I like to think of it as appreciating the finer things in life," I sparred and she propped her arms under her breasts, giving them an extra boost. All I could do was groan. "I'm glad the hotel isn't filled with kids. I'm a little surprised since it is Minnesota Educators Association weekend."

"I saw some earlier, but it's late and most are back in their rooms. I want you to tell me something I don't know about you."

She lifted one brow and chewed on her lower lip, thinking. "I don't like going to church, but I do it for my kids."

"Well, there's a loaded statement straight out of the gate," I said, tongue in cheek.

"Do you go to church?" she asked and I shook my head no.

"I grew up Catholic, but I have a hard time with most of what they believe in. That doesn't mean I don't believe. Why don't you like to go? Is it because of Jacob?"

She scooped water up over her arms and closed her eyes. "You know, I could get used to being in the water again. I really like this. I should find out if the community center has a chair lift."

"They don't, but they have a beach chair they use to get people in and out of the pool."

She frowned. "That's okay for kids and the elderly, but I'm not sure I like that."

Okay, so she didn't want to talk about it. I'd let it go rather than ruin the fun we were having. "Can I ask you a question?"

She motioned at me. "I haven't been able to stop you all day," she said, tongue in cheek.

I caressed her legs under the water. "How come your lower legs are so thin?"

"Wearing the sockets around them shrinks the tissue and muscles down. That's one of the reasons the legs need to be made smaller every so often. It's just the nature of the human body. Since I don't have feet, I can't build the muscles the way normal people would, and even if I could, it would be counterintuitive since they're in the sockets all day. I work at staying limber and that's all I can do."

"Is that something I can watch?"

She rolled her eyes. "You know, if you keep this up, Santa is going to put you on his naughty list."

"Well, when you have a name like Nick Klaus, you get an exception," I explained in a teacherish tone of voice.

"And you do take Christmas very seriously. Maybe you are Santa Claus. I've heard things around town about what you do besides playing Santa at the community event."

I raised a brow and shook my head. "No, that's pretty much what I do." She stared at me long and hard until I sighed. "Fine, okay, so I spend every Sunday morning doing all the paperwork to get grants for the Coats for Kids Christmas program. When I moved to Snowberry, I heard about it through school. I discovered they missed out on money available to help the program because they didn't have anyone to write the grants and submit the paperwork. I also chair the actual Coats for Kids event."

"That sort of sounds like something Santa would do." She was teasing, and I rubbed her leg under the water.

"Being Santa is the best part, and I hope, in some small way, it helps."

She cocked her head. "I would think that seeing kids warm and happy all winter long would show you that it helps in a big way. You understand people, and you don't make them feel bad for situations out of their control."

"I understand people?" I asked, shifting to her side of the tub and taking her hand.

"Yeah, you understand people, sometimes in ways they don't understand themselves. Look at how you managed the situation with Xander, and how Ben seeks you out to help him work through how he is feeling. The same can be said about grant writing. You have an understanding of the process, of course, but more importantly, you grasp the mission statement of the program. You recognize the practical side of kids needing coats in Minnesota, but also the emotional side of kids wanting to look good, and feel good, about themselves, even if their parents struggle to provide for them. You understand that a new coat can build these kids' self-esteem and make them better students, and eventually better members of the community."

I leaned in and kissed her lips briefly, though I wanted it to last forever. "I never looked at it that way, but it makes me happy in ways you don't understand to hear you say those things about me. I've felt like you've barely tolerated me for the last five years. Know that what you just said means more to me than you'll probably ever understand."

She scooted away and looked me up and down. "Barely tolerated you? What are you talking about?"

I didn't want to have this conversation here. Not when we were enjoying the warm water, and I could be enjoying her warm lips. I reached for her and pulled her to me by her waist. She gazed up into my face and her lashes held droplets of water that made her eyes look sweet and dewy. Her hair was damp and starting to curl around her shoulders in perfect waves and I wondered what it would feel like to run my fingers through it as I made love to her.

"I asked you a question, Nick," she said, her voice slightly more breathless than the last time.

I pulled her onto my lap and cradled her in my arms. "Shut up and kiss me, Mands."

I climbed off the terribly uncomfortable couch and bent over, touching my toes. My back was killing me and I groaned when I glanced at the clock on the microwave. It was only one a.m. That meant too many more hours of torture on that thing. I quietly tiptoed to the bathroom and noticed a light shining under the door to the bedroom. I had insisted she take the bedroom, even though it had two separate beds just so she had some time and space of her own. But why was the light still on at one a.m.?

I flushed and washed, going so far as using some mouthwash before I shut the bathroom light off. I hesitated by the bedroom door. Should I check on her? Maybe she fell asleep with the light on and I should shut it off? Maybe she sleeps with the light on? Maybe I should just knock and see if she responds? Maybe I should stop acting like a sixteen-year-old boy and be a man?

I pushed the handle down on the door until it clicked open and then I stuck my head inside carefully. She was sitting on the bed farthest from the door, her head bent over and her hands moving on the bed like she was playing cards. I could hear her humming, and then it hit me, she was playing the piano. She must have heard me at that moment because she turned and put her hand over her heart.

"You scared me, Nick."

I pushed the door open the rest of the way. "I'm sorry, that wasn't my intention. I saw the light on when I went to the bathroom and wanted to check on you. Why aren't you sleeping?"

I approached the bed she was sitting on and saw the roll out piano she was using. It was made of plastic, but all the keys were there in black and white.

"I'm nervous about tomorrow, so I was practicing my pieces. I'm sorry if I woke you, I thought I had it turned down low enough."

I knelt by the bed and rubbed her back. She was wearing a thin satiny nightgown, the long sleeves ending at her wrists in soft lace, and the front teasing me every time she bent forward.

"Your piano didn't wake me. That bed out there is a monster." I pointed at the piano, "This thing really works?"

She nodded and tapped out a short run from

The Cups song. I laid a kiss on her shoulder through the material. "I'm going to miss you when you're gone."

It was as though she didn't hear me. She started rolling the keyboard up and straightening her papers. "I'll go to bed now."

I stilled her hands. "Why are you so nervous? You've done lots of presentations like this."

"I have, but this one is a professional development presentation, so teachers are going to be attending for credit. I have to be on point and it has to be informative and applicable to each individual classroom."

"Okay, but if you don't get some sleep before you present, it's not going to be informative. You'll be too tired. I have the utmost confidence in you, or I wouldn't have submitted your name as a presenter for the course. Just take a deep breath and remember this is going to be a piece of cake. You love teaching music and it will show in your presentation."

"Wait, you submitted my name?" she asked, turning toward me. I could see her breasts through the material of her nightgown and I groaned but covered it with a cough. She wasn't wearing a bra and it was all I could do to keep from reaching out to caress them.

"You had to know someone submitted your name," I said, my eyes glued to her face. It was the only way to keep my mind from wandering to the forbidden fruit.

She threw her hand up a little. "I thought it was Neal."

"Does it matter who submitted your name? I got the info sheet, called Neal and asked his opinion. We both agreed you were the woman for the job."

She looked down at her hands. "Why did you say that earlier? That I barely tolerated you the last five years."

I chuckled and shook my head. "I wish I could take that back, but since I said it, I'll answer. You were standoffish whenever we saw each other at home. You were always professional and courteous at school, at least when the kids were around, and you weren't crying at the piano bench." I winked and she rolled her eyes toward the ceiling for a moment. "But it seemed like you were afraid of me or afraid of getting close to me. You let the kids come over, but you turned down every offer I made for anything social. I didn't have all the information I needed to really know why, but I understand now."

She gazed up at me and her eyes were the most honest I had ever seen them. "I was hurt all the way to my soul, Nick. When you moved in next door, it had only been a year since Jacob's betrayal. I was scared of men, but more than that, I was scared to look weak. I had to prove that I could raise my kids without a man, and I could do it even without feet." She smacked herself in the forehead and shook her head. "That sounded so stupid."

I rubbed the spot on her head that she had hit and shook my head. "No, it didn't sound stupid. You were determined to show everyone, including your father, that you could do it alone, even though you had challenges most single moms don't face."

"Yeah, exactly. It wasn't that I didn't like you; just the opposite was true. I liked you too much, and I knew if I let myself lean on you, then I wouldn't stand on my own two fake feet and make a life for my children."

I snickered and caressed her cheek. "I love how you poke fun at yourself in a way that is endearing. Don't you see that you have made a life for your children? Your kids are smart, kind, beautiful souls who have more empathy for their friends than any other kids I have ever met before. That's because you've taught them how to be that way just by being you."

She shrugged without confidence. "Sometimes I think Ben has had to grow up too fast. He feels like he has to take care of me. He was so mad at me when he got home and found out I had the blister. He scolded me about not taking care of myself and then insisted I stay on the couch while he fixed Esther's supper and got her ready for bed. I felt like I hadn't accomplished anything by being so stubborn."

I moved the papers, so I could sit next to her on the bed. "Don't you see, Mandy? You accomplished way more than you set out to accomplish. Not only did you raise those two kids alone for years, but you raised them to be independent and loving in ways a lot of parents don't these days. What eleven-year-old boy would take on the responsibility of taking care of his sister without stomping around and acting put out? Yours, because you've shown him that being loving and kind is the right way to live."

"I hadn't thought of it that way."

"Ben is going to become a man of great conviction because of the way you've raised him. Esther is going to be a smart, strong-willed, independent woman because she's had you for a role model all these years. Don't ever, ever underestimate the kind of job you've done with them."

She nodded quickly, and I know it was to fight back the tears that waited at the edge of her lashes. "I hope so. They're the innocent victims of my mistakes. If I had listened to my gut and not married Jacob, I wouldn't have screwed my life up so terribly."

I stroked her cheek with my thumb and smiled. "And you wouldn't have Ben and Esther."

She gave me the palms up. "I'm so out of my depth with you, Nick. How can you still be single when you're as wonderful as you are?"

"The truth is, five years ago, I saw the most beautiful woman standing in her yard laughing at her little girl who was toddling around the yard, and instantly, no one could ever measure up to her."

She laid her hand on my chest and let it fall down the length of my t-shirt. "You're just saying that."

"I wish I was. If I was just saying it, then I wouldn't have lain in bed alone every night for the last five years. If I was just saying it, I would have a string of women coming and going from my life, but I haven't, have I?"

"Not that I've seen," she whispered.

"And you won't see that. Frankly, there's only one woman I want. If it takes me another five years to convince her of that, then so be it."

"Nick …" she started, and I held my finger to her lips.

"I know you think because we work together, it's problematic to ever be more than colleagues, but it's not. If my job is the only thing keeping you from exploring how we feel right now, then I'll find a new one."

Her head snapped up and her eyes widened. "You can't leave Snowberry!"

"But I would, Mandy. Maybe, in the end, I'll leave Snowberry anyway. There's only so long a man can live next door to the woman he knows is perfect for him, and not do something about it."

"Are you doing something about it? Now, I mean."

I glanced around the room and then back to her. The front of her nightgown beckoned me and I leaned forward, laying a kiss at the top of the lace. "I guess I am. At least by being honest about how

I feel." I leaned back and caressed her chest slowly. "It's awfully damn freeing, too."

"What's that like? To be free? I don't know what that even feels like," she whispered.

I leaned in and kissed her, laying her back against the bed, the paper crinkling under our weight as I lay next to her. My lips left hers to kiss the length of her jawline to her ear, where I rested my mouth. "Do you want to find out what it feels like? I can teach you," I whispered, and felt her shudder under me.

"It's been so long," she moaned softly, arching under me, "but I'm afraid to do something we can never take back."

I laid one more kiss on her neck and then sat up, running my hand down her arm, smiling as I stood. My desires were blatantly obvious inside my now tented boxer shorts, but I didn't hide it, for what would be the point.

"It's time for bed, Mands. I'll see you in the morning," I promised, going to the door and turning off the light. The room faded into darkness except for the light filtering through the curtains.

"Nick, you should sleep in the other bed, so you can rest. You said the sofa bed was a monster."

I was next to the bed in two steps, leaning over, so I could lay my lips near her ear. "I don't think that's a good idea. I'm so hard right now I'm in physical pain. Lying next to you all night is only going to be self-inflicted torture that even the sofa bed can't stand up to."

"Nick, I'm scared."

I straightened, forcing my feet back to the doorway. "I know you are, Mands, I'm just not sure of what."

"I don't know either."

"When you figure out what you're afraid of, I'll be here. In the meantime, don't expect me to go anywhere. I'm rather attached to your gorgeous blue eyes."

I opened the door and left the room before I lost my nerve.

Chapter Twelve

I sank back down onto the sofa bed and put my head in my hands. What was I doing wrong? What wasn't I saying that would convince her I wanted to be part of her life? I slid my legs under the blankets and rolled to my side. Something told me saying *I love you* wasn't a smart idea, even if it was true. You don't walk around with four degrees in your pocket and not see what's right in front of your face. I love her, but I can't tell her that right now. It would only serve to scare her more.

As much as I want, and need, to be with her, it has to be on her terms. She has to come to me and show me she's ready to take the next step. I didn't lie to her, though. I can't stay in Snowberry and live next to her forever if I can't have her.

For the last five years, I've told myself I was gaining her trust and getting to know her, but now that reasoning falls flat. I know her and I love her. Anything that happens now has to be because she wants it and initiates it. I respect her honesty and her fear, but with each passing day, I feel time slipping away. I've known all along her curt attitude wasn't disdain for me as a person, but rather fear.

She was afraid of letting me get close to her because I'm a man.

I heard the door to the bedroom open and my thoughts froze instantly. Was she going to the bathroom?

"Nick?" she whisper-asked and I sat up in the bed. She stood in front of me, wobbling on her crutches. I was out of the bed and had her in my arms just as she started to fall over.

"Where are your legs, love?" I asked, cradling her in my arms as I walked back to the bedroom.

"I didn't want to take the time to put them on. I wanted you to hold me in your arms again."

I smiled down at her skeptically. "Mission accomplished."

She reached up and laid her hand on my cheek. I turned my head and kissed her palm, the sweet scent of her pineapple lotion assailing my nose.

"You're going to hurt yourself doing that," I scolded, laying her down on the bed and kneeling in front of it.

"At least I would feel something other than how I'm feeling right now, Nick."

"Fear?" I asked, and she shook her head.

"I don't think so. I think it's more like self-hatred. I'm not afraid to be with you, I'm afraid to let you see me."

"Why?" I asked, rubbing her right leg up and down. Her soft skin was warm and her nightgown cool. It was almost too much for my senses.

"I've only been with one man, Nick," she explained.

"Jacob," I said and she nodded.

"He left me because I wasn't perfect. He sent the message loud and clear when the woman he had bent over my couch was a perfect Barbie doll. I've spent a lot of time convincing myself it's easier to be alone than to risk being with a man ever again. When I'm with you, I can't convince myself it's a bad idea to let you love every part of me."

I rested my hand on her belly, over her nightgown. "What does that tell you?"

"That's the part that has me confused. Is it just my libido getting the better of me, or is it something more?"

"If I ask you a question, will you answer it honestly and not punch me?" She nodded and I took her hand, lest she lies to me about the punching part. "When you use your toys, do you think about me?" She nodded once and that simple admittance was as good as a punch to the solar plexus. I could barely breathe but forced myself to ask the next question. "After you're done, and you're lying in bed alone, are you satisfied?"

"Just the opposite, I feel so alone that I cry myself to sleep."

"Oh, love," I whispered, climbing next to her and pulling her into my arms, resting her head on my chest. "To hear you say that it breaks my heart. I promise you, the first time we make love, you'll fall asleep in my arms."

She gazed up at me. "Prove it."

I groaned and my lower half tighten at her words. "That's a dangerous thing to say, Mands. I have an extremely hard time being challenged and not carrying through."

She ran her hand over my chest and I closed my eyes, swallowing hard. "You won't hurt me, I know that. You've already seen my legs and you're still lying here. I don't have anything to worry about."

I leaned down and kissed her softly until her lips parted. She sighed when my tongue toured every part of her mouth. "Who are you trying to convince, you or me?"

I let my hand fall from her shoulder and rest alongside her breast, rubbing across her ribs until her breath caught.

"I don't need to convince myself. I need to remind myself. If I don't, I'll be an eighty-year-old woman with a whole lot of regrets."

I let my hand move away from the side of her breast and across the front, taking pleasure in how she pressed into my hand, making me feel her hardened nipple against my palm. It was when I felt her hand through the material of my boxers that I groaned, my senses finally returning.

I stilled her hand, holding it to me. "We can't do this. I didn't come prepared."

"Doesn't every guy have a condom in their wallet?" she asked, surprised.

"Not this guy. This guy hadn't gotten past the part where you talked to him without running at the first word out of his mouth."

She closed her eyes and shook her head. "It wasn't you."

"I know," I promised, kissing her lips one last time and then sitting up.

She grabbed my hand and held me in place. "We don't need condoms. I had an IUD placed after Esther was born. I never had it taken out because I was too embarrassed. It's good for a few more years."

"I'm having trouble forming a sentence," I admitted and she laughed softly, massaging me through the ridiculously thin material covering me. I could feel the heat of her hand and I wanted nothing between us.

"Maybe you should talk less, Mr. Klaus," she suggested.

I flipped her over in one motion, laying her on the bed, and placed one knee between her legs. "I can think of a dozen other ways to keep my mouth busy."

She squirmed under me and brought one leg up to rub across the front of my boxers. I held her hands above her head and laid over her gently, kissing her lips until her body softened under me.

I pulled my lips from hers and gazed down at her in the low light. "Let me be clear before I lose any ability to think. If at any time, you want me to stop, all you have to do is say the word and I will."

I moved my lips down her neck while my hands bunched up the nightgown. I pulled it out from under her and over her head, dropping it to the floor by the bed. She lay before me naked and I grew even harder. "You're absolutely gorgeous," I whispered, letting her pull my t-shirt over my head. I stopped her hands at my boxers and shook my head.

"I'm going to make you feel good, first," I promised and she let her hands fall to the bed. I took my time kissing, sucking, and massaging every part of her. My lips lingered on one nipple until she started to squirm beneath my lips, and then I eased off, switching to the other one to repeat the game. While my lips sucked at her tender flesh, my hand found her mound, wet and waiting for me. She cried out when I touched her and I froze.

"Are you okay?" I asked.

"Please don't stop," she begged.

I smiled, kissing her lips as I showed her how to be loved. When she moaned against them, I nearly lost myself as it reverberated inside my head.

"I want to touch you," she said, hooking her thumbs in the waistband of my boxers and pulling them down. When they didn't come off, she stared up at me.

I smiled reassuringly. "I'm a little too excited," I winked and leaned back, removing the offending garment and letting it meet the same fate as her nightgown.

She reached out and ran a finger down my length. It was pure heaven in a way I had never felt before. This was what real, life-changing love felt like. I closed my eyes, trying to slow my breathing as her hand encircled me, tugging me toward her. I leaned down and kissed her, my lips becoming more demanding and my moans more passionate the longer she held me.

"Please, Nick," she said against my lips. "Don't make me wait any longer."

I lay over her, my hands in her hair, and my face just inches from hers. "Are you sure? We can never go back after tonight if I make love to you."

She nodded and her eyes reflected my desire. "I don't want to go back. This feels too good."

I lowered myself the rest of the way and lifted her one leg, wrapping it around my waist. Then, using every last bit of patience I had, slowly slipped inside her. "Oh, Mandy," I moaned when I thought I was buried all the way inside her. She pushed forward against me and it was then that I knew nothing would ever be the same.

The breakfast nook was busy, but the choices were endless, so I didn't blame people for taking their time. Made to order omelets, waffles, meat, and fruit barely touched the offerings. Mandy was at the table with her plate and I carried two mugs of coffee over then went back for my omelet. I was feeling the effects of a fantastic night of very little sleep. We didn't rest for more than half an hour before we were kissing or caressing each other again.

By three a.m. we were both so exhausted we fell asleep in each other's arms, and when I woke up this morning, she was still there. She conceded I had definitely proved I could satisfy her the way I promised.

"Well, it looks like the rumors are true," I heard as I approached the table. Cindy Arsenault, our first-grade busybody, stood over Mandy, her arms folded and her *I gotcha look* firmly planted on her face.

I slid into my seat and set my plate down.

"What rumors?" Mandy asked calmly in a way only a well-seasoned teacher could.

Cindy motioned between us. "Word on the street is, the teacher and boss are over here shaking it up."

I glanced up at her. "And you came over to find out?"

"Don't flatter yourself. I'm staying here because they didn't have a room at the Holiday Inn. I saw you two rather cozy in the hot tub last night. How hot did it get? Were you a good little schoolgirl for Mr. Principal?"

I pushed my chair back and was leaning on the table in Cindy's face by the time Mandy grabbed my arm, forcing me back into my chair.

"First of all, Cindy," Mandy said, her voice dripping with honey, "we live in Snowberry, not Chicago. There is no such thing as *word on the street*."

She used her long, sweet fingers to make quotes around it and I remembered how they felt on my skin last night. "That's simply another way for you to not claim ownership of the crude rumors you start. Second of all, he's not my boss. Neal Newsom is my boss, which means Nick and I are colleagues, and next-door neighbors. There is no boss to teacher disciplinary situation that will arise. What we choose to do outside of school is really none of your damn business."

Cindy clucked her tongue and shook her head. "My, we are kind of defensive this morning, aren't we? It's nice to see you looking so," she waved her hand around Mandy again, "relaxed."

I had enough of the whole thing and stood, leaning over the table in a pose she could mistake as nothing other than what it was, authority. "What you need to understand, Cindy, is that while I am not Mandy's boss, I am yours, and you are crossing the line into insubordination at an incredible speed."

She crossed her arms and faced me like a defiant child. "Look around you, Nick, we aren't at school. This is no different than if we were in Snowberry and I found the two of you smooching in a booth at Gallo's."

I flipped the name badge around that hung on my neck and held it up to her face. "You see this? It indicates I'm presenting at the conference as Principal Nick Klaus. That means this is a school event. According to the contract you signed, any event, in the school building or out of it, requires you to conduct yourself in a manner that exemplifies professionalism. As far as I'm concerned, you're not."

"Are you going to write me up? Because bedding a teacher in the school you run doesn't seem exemplarily professional to me."

I stood and took her arm, guiding her away from the table. "I don't care what your opinion is, Cindy. The fact is, I have a two-room suite and Mandy is sharing it to conserve costs. You can think anything you like, but that doesn't make it true. Now, if you'll excuse me, I need to finish my breakfast before my speech."

I turned back to the table and Mandy was gone. I ran a hand through my hair and cursed inwardly. Cindy was, and always would be, a rumormonger. I grabbed a to-go box and dumped my omelet in it, adding some bagels and donuts, then grabbed two to-go cups of coffee and hightailed it to the elevator. I didn't know what I would find when I got to the room, but chances were, she would be on her way out. I kicked the side of the elevator in frustration. Last night was the best night of my life, and that woman just blew it all apart in under two minutes.

I barely waited for the doors to finish opening before I pushed through them and walked the hallway to the room. I took deep breaths, forcing my anger at Cindy down so I could concentrate on Mandy. I slipped the key into the lock and opened the door with my butt, bringing the food to the bar and leaving it there. I leaned against the bedroom door and watched her throwing clothes into her suitcase. She turned, headed for the bathroom and ran straight into me. I grabbed her arms and held her still, then tucked her into a hug, even though she was stiff as a board.

"Let me go, Nick," she demanded, but I didn't loosen my grip.

"Where are you going to go, Mandy? I drove us here and we both have a presentation to give in a few hours."

"I can't do that now. I need to go home," she cried.

I walked her backward to the bed and sat her down, then kneeled between her knees.

"Mandy, look at me," I ordered, but her eyes remained downcast at the floor. I waited patiently, my years of holding out for the most stubborn of kids coming in handy. Finally, she met my eyes.

"I want to be very clear with you that there is nothing unprofessional about us being together, morally or otherwise."

She pointed toward the door and beyond. "Maybe she's right. Maybe being together is wrong."

I brought my lips down on hers with all the pent-up frustration and want I still had inside me. I didn't take it slow and I didn't take it easy. I bit down on her lip, holding it until I heard her moan softly and then sucked it gently until her arms came up around my neck, holding me to her.

I plunged my tongue between her lips and dominated her mouth until she gave me all the control. My pants were tented and tight and I wanted her more at that moment than I ever had. Without breaking the kiss, I pulled her one hand down and settled it over my desire, moaning into her mouth when she cupped me and caressed me.

I pulled my lips away and rested my forehead against hers. "Did that feel wrong?"

She lowered her head and rested her forehead against my chest, wrapping her arms around my back. "That's the hard part, it doesn't feel wrong. I've never felt the way I do when you kiss me. Not even with Jacob. It feels right. It feels the way I think love is supposed to feel. It feels like you accept me for everything I am and everything I'm not."

I laid my lips on her temple and kissed her softly. "I do, don't you see. That's why I'm left to wonder why you're letting someone like Cindy ruin that feeling?"

"I'm embarrassed that people think that about us, aren't you?"

I laughed softly and squeezed her tightly. "Not in the least. Cindy is a busybody and her *word on the street* is nothing more than the voices in her head. Do you know anyone else in that school who would talk behind our backs about us seeing each other? Can you think of anyone who would care?"

She shook her head no. "I can think of a lot of people who would care, but in a good way. They would be excited to know we're seeing each other."

"Exactly. You have to ignore Cindy and go about your day, including giving your presentation."

"Is that what we are doing, Nick? Seeing each other?"

I held her out away from me and gave her a questionable smile. "I'm seeing you in front of me right now, aren't I?"

"You have taken me to dinner twice and made love to me once."

I peeked up at her from under my brow. "Only once?"

"Let me rephrase that. You've made love to me multiple times in one night."

I kissed her again with a naughty grin. "And I'm going to make it two for two tonight, but first, we have some work to do."

She glanced at the suitcase on the bed and back to me. I shook my head and squeezed her hands. "The only place you're going is to the River Centre. You have no reason to be embarrassed. You're a grown woman and can see whomever you want to see. Personally, I'm going to walk into my presentation with a goofy smile on my face and my chest puffed out because I know the most beautiful woman in the world will be waiting for me when I'm done. You will be waiting, right?"

She nodded slowly. "You have to give me time to get used to this. It's all new to me. I've never been with a man who cares about my feelings before."

I caressed her cheek and kissed her again for good measure. "Then he wasn't the right man for you. The right man cares about your feelings more than his own. If you had insisted on going home, I would have taken you, and not cared about the repercussions, but I had to know why you were running. Was it that you were ashamed we were together? Or was it because it scared you to think about the world outside these walls knowing about us?"

"I don't care what Cindy thinks. She has called me an entitled cripple since the accident. This," she motioned back and forth between us, "feels really good, and I don't want the world out there to tell me it's not."

I laid a kiss on her chest just above the swell of her breast. "I've been waiting five years to feel like this and I won't let anyone ruin it for either of us."

"I'll try not to, but I can't promise I won't worry. I will."

"Does Cindy really call you that and does she do it in school?" I asked, trying to keep my temper in check.

Her eyes immediately went down to the floor and I knew the answer. "Please, don't make a big deal about it, Nick."

"Why do you put up with that? She doesn't have the right to be a bully any more than Xander does."

"It's easier than drawing attention to myself,

and she doesn't do it where anyone else can hear her."

"You know what's going to happen if I ever hear her say that, right?"

She nodded. "I'm pretty sure she's barely employed as it is. I've heard she's nearly used up her strikes."

"Well, that word on the street is accurate. I could use today as her final strike, but I would rather make sure I have enough proof, so there is no way she can weasel out of the accusation. I'm serious, though. Don't put up with that crap. Either get up and leave, or tell her where to stick it, but do not let her get in here." I tapped her temple and she nodded, sitting up a little straighter.

"You're right. I'm going to go out there and do what I came here to do and to hell with Cindy." She froze and her body filled with tension. "What if she's at the presentation? It counts toward professional development."

I pushed myself up off my knees and pulled her from the bed and into the small bar area. I sat her down on a barstool and set a cup of coffee in front of her. I heated up the food in the microwave, then split the omelet onto two plates and placed one in front of her, leaning against the counter.

"Eat that. You need food in you before we go. As far as Cindy being there, I hope she is."

She already had a bite of eggs in her mouth, so she lifted a brow until she swallowed. "You enjoy torturing me?"

I stabbed a piece of egg and smiled out of one side of my mouth. "Only in bed. But if she shows up today, text me. I'll sit in the back and wait for her to screw up. When she does, I'll be there to witness it. You know the old saying?" She shook her head and I grinned. "Three strikes and you're out." I popped the eggs in my mouth and chewed while she tried not to laugh aloud.

Chapter Thirteen

I could see Mandy outside the doors of the center looking at her phone. I stepped out into the cool autumn air and glanced around. No one I knew was within visual distance, so I snaked my arms around her waist. "Hey, sex—" Her elbow landed in my ribs and I grunted instead of finishing the word. She spun and I grabbed her arm as she was ready to roundhouse me in the jaw. "Mandy, it's me!" I shouted louder than I wanted, but it got her attention.

"Oh my gosh, Nick! What were you thinking?" She swatted me on the back of the head as she yelled. Now I was rubbing the back of my head *and* my gut.

"I was thinking I wanted to give you a hug," I said, winded from the elbow in my ribs.

She led me to a small bench and I sat. "Not smart to come up behind a woman in a big city. You can get away with it in Snowberry, but not here."

I rubbed my head. "I'm starting to see that. Did you take self-defense courses or something?"

It was her turn to grunt in a half-snorting

manner. "I have brothers. I don't need self-defense classes."

I held up my hand for a small high five. "You win that round," I chuckled.

"Are you okay, or did I really hurt you?" She was worried and wrung her hands together as though trying to figure out what to do.

"I'm fine," I insisted as she sat next to me. "I saw you looking at your phone. Did you hear from the kids?"

She nodded. "Esther is helping her grandma with the wedding decorations and Ben is helping Jacob get the grounds ready, which I'm quite surprised about." She held up the phone and Ben was waving back in the picture. He didn't look like he was having too much fun, in my opinion.

"Why does that surprise you?"

She shrugged and tucked the phone back in her purse. "Jacob usually doesn't spend much time with Ben when he's there. I'm not sure why."

I stood and pulled her up, then put my arm around her shoulders. "I might know why."

She glanced up at me and raised one brow, "Do you have a psychology degree, too?"

I smiled and squeezed her shoulder. "I don't need one. Remember when I told you Ben came over last week and talked with me? He told me he had a tough time forgiving his dad for what he did to your family. He said he thinks Jacob is hypocritical to do what he's done and then to stand in a church and tell others not to do it."

"Jacob is a hypocrite. I thought he was too young to fully comprehend what happened. I had no idea he harbors that kind of resentment towards him."

"He doesn't want you to know because you deal with enough, but he hates going to Jacob's. He knows he has to go because of the court, but he also doesn't want to send Esther by herself. I think he's very …" I held my hand to my belly and punched it a few times, "full of turmoil, I guess. He's at that age where he's starting to become aware of his own emotions and how they affect his life. What he used to be able to put aside as a youngster as of no concern to him, has suddenly become very concerning. He's seeing how Jacob's choices have had a spiral effect on everyone, and he's afraid of doing the same thing. All he needs is reassurance that you understand and that you're willing to listen to him, and his concerns."

She hung her head and then dropped it into her hand. "Dammit, I hate this. I want him to be a kid, not worried about things he can't control. I'll talk to him when he gets home."

I kissed her cheek as we walked toward the hotel. "I think that's the best thing you can do. How was your presentation? I haven't seen you all day."

With the mention of her work, the gloomy cloud lifted and she smiled brightly. "It was so much fun! It was standing room only and the group was engaged and enthusiastic about ways to integrate music into the classroom. Many of the teachers weren't there because music education had fallen to them, but because they wanted to find ways to teach the kids using music, which is something kids always respond to."

"That's great news. It's nice to see teachers innovating and finding ways to use music to teach everyday techniques. Of course, I know you rocked it because I was there for part of it. You couldn't see me, but I was there."

She stumbled and I caught her before she fell. "What do you mean you were there?"

"I stopped in to make sure Cindy hadn't shown up. I know you well enough to know you wouldn't text me if she had, because you might be interrupting me."

She laughed softly and laid her head on my shoulder for a second. "You might be right, but she wasn't there."

"That's probably because I saw her shortly before it started and warned her not to even think about going to your conference."

"That wouldn't have stopped her if she wanted to," she quipped.

"Oh, I know. Which is why I had to check. She wasn't there, but you were playing beautiful music and I needed that to get through the rest of those boring seminars."

I was following her through the revolving door when her phone rang. She stepped to the side and answered it.

"Hey, Ben, I just got your picture, looks like you're working hard."

She was silent for a moment and then waved her hand. "Ben, Ben, slow down. What's going on?" she asked calmly, but I heard the little bit of fear in her voice. I led her to a leather sofa and sat next to her.

"That's ridiculous, Ben. He knows he can." She paused again and then pounded her fist on her leg. "Put your father on the phone."

I tried not to listen in on the conversation, but it was difficult at best as she radiated anger and fear. I rubbed her knee, anxiety filling me when I felt it trembling. She wasn't angry as much as she was scared. She spoke briefly with Jacob and whatever he said, she didn't like it. She finally covered the mouthpiece. "How soon can we be to Rochester?"

"It's only about an hour," I said and she uncovered the phone.

"I'll be there in ninety minutes. Put Ben back on the line."

She waited and I rubbed her back until she started speaking again and then my hand froze in its spot.

"Ben, listen, I'm coming to get you and Esther. I need you to stay with her until I get there. Is she on the couch?" She nodded at whatever he said. "Okay, good. Now I want you to keep ice on it until I get there. Change it as you need to, but don't take the ice off. It will hurt less that way. Dad said that you gave her some Advil, which is good. You can let her have sips of water, but no food, okay?" She waited for his response and then stood. "I'm going to get my things and Nick and I will be there as quick as we can." I heard an excited voice on the other line. "Yes, we rode together since we were both presenting." More excited chatter and I was already moving us toward the front desk. "No, Ben, stop. We're done with our seminars and you aren't bothering us. Just stay with your sister and we will be there soon. I love you." She waited for a response and then clicked the off button.

"Esther fell playing at her grandma's and hurt her arm. Ben thinks it's broken, but Jacob is refusing to take her to the ER. Says he doesn't have insurance."

"You carry the insurance on the kids, Mands," I said, confused.

"Exactly! And he knows that!" she exclaimed, throwing her arms up.

I grabbed them and held her. "Did you tell him to take her?"

"I did, but he's refusing, says he doesn't have time and his mom and dad have to go to work. He thinks it's only sprained and it will be fine. He was actually going to wait until after the wedding if you can believe that."

My blood pressure started to rise. "I will believe just about anything when it comes to that guy."

"Ben says her arm is swollen and looks to be at a funny angle. He thinks it's broken, but she's sleeping after he gave her some Advil. My eleven-year-old had to get her ice and Advil because no one could help an innocent third grader. I'm so angry right now."

I turned her toward the room. "I'm not doing much better. Go get your things packed and I'll check out and be up to get our bags. We can be there in an hour, tops."

She froze. "You can't leave! You have more seminars tomorrow."

"Mandy," I said calmly, not wanting to take my anger out on her. "There is no seminar more important than Esther. Go get our things ready, I'm taking you to her."

She turned and walked quickly toward the elevator and I took three deep breaths before I turned to the receptionist to check us out.

Mandy pointed at the third house on the street. "That's his place."

I pulled the car to the curb and turned the engine off. She was already out the door before I could get my seatbelt off. I made the drive in under an hour, thankful no cops were on the road. I helped her up the three porch steps and she didn't even knock, just opened the door and stormed in.

"Ben, I'm here!" she called and he came skidding out of an old-fashioned archway and right into her. I grabbed her before he knocked them down.

"Mom, I'm so glad you came. She says it really hurts and she won't stop crying."

We followed him into the living room where Esther lay on the couch, sniffing and cradling her arm. Mandy was by her side instantly and pushing the wet, sweaty hair off her face.

"It's okay, baby. Mommy's here. I'm going to take you to the doctor, so your arm stops hurting."

Esther whimpered almost as though she couldn't speak. Mandy glanced up at Ben. "Where is your father?"

"He's in the backyard. I told him you were coming and that's the last I've seen of him."

She turned to me. "Nick, would you have Ben sit in the backseat and then bring Esther out and rest her on his lap. The hospital is only a mile and we can make it without worrying about seatbelts. I need to let their father know I'm taking them."

"Of course," I promised, kneeling next to Esther and giving her a hand up. "I'm going to carry you to the car, okay, Esther?" I asked and the little girl nodded, big crocodile tears in her eyes. "Thank you for bringing my mommy, Nick," she said. Her little voice was hoarse from crying and it broke my heart. It also ramped up Mandy's anger.

A man came through the door from the kitchen and stopped in his tracks. "Who are you?" he asked as I held Esther in my arms.

"I'm Nick Klaus. I'm the principal at the kids' school. I was at an educators' event with Mandy when Ben called."

Jacob rolled his eyes. "You're all overreacting. She's being a drama queen and will be fine by morning."

Mandy was on top of him in less than one second and there was nothing I could do with Esther in my arms.

She stuck her finger in his chest and got up in his face. "How dare you say that about your own daughter! She's eight, not eighteen, and you have no right to act as if she's putting you out. You wanted her here to start with. I will take her to the hospital, since you're clearly way too busy to take your child's welfare into account, and let a medical doctor be the judge of how dramatic she is being." She turned on her heel and grabbed Ben's arm, pushing him out the door.

"Are you my ex-wife's newest booty call?" Jacob asked from behind me.

I turned on my heel in one motion. "I don't think that's really any of your business, Jacob, considering how you've treated her. Now, since you're far too busy to tend to your daughter's injuries, I'm going to."

I left the room with Esther and she laid her head on my chest as though she knew the battle had finally been won.

Chapter Fourteen

"I brought you something to eat, Ben," I said as I approached him. He was sitting on a couch in the family waiting room while Mandy spoke with the doctor about Esther's arm.

He glanced up and I handed him a sandwich and a can of pop. "Thanks, Nick, I shouldn't be hungry, but I am."

"Why shouldn't you be hungry?" I asked, sitting next to him.

He shrugged. "Esther is hurt and I should have been there."

"Ben, you know this isn't your fault, right? Kids fall every day. It's part of growing up."

"If she fell," he said around the sandwich in his mouth. He took two more bites without swallowing the first and I watched, surprised. When he did finally swallow, I put my hand on his shoulder.

"When was the last time you ate, Ben?"

He shrugged and took another big bite so he couldn't talk. I waited him out and then held his arm down, so he couldn't take another bite and gave him my principal stare.

"Last night. Dad didn't feed us today. I was

going to get something after we finished with the yard, but then Grandma brought Esther over."

"Did Esther get breakfast and lunch?"

"Probably. When we stay with Grandma, she always feeds us, but when we stay with dad, it's hit or miss unless I cook something."

I stored that away for later when Mandy was on more stable ground. "You said *if she fell*, what did you mean by that?"

"Sometimes Tasha's kids are mean to her. She told me Tasha's son, Devon, pushed her when they were playing. I'm sure he didn't purposely mean to hurt her."

"Will Esther tell your mom that Devon did this?"

He stared at me and shook his head slightly. "About as likely as her telling mom about Xander, but I won't keep quiet this time."

I patted his back. "Good thinking. If someone hurt her on purpose, there will be hell to pay."

"Are you and my mom dating?" he asked suddenly, as though he couldn't hold the question in any longer.

"We are. Why do you ask?"

He laid his head back on the couch. "I just wondered. I didn't want to walk into the house and be surprised by the two of you naked."

I leaned forward and took his shoulders. "Ben, I want you to understand something right now. You will never come home and find your mother and me naked. I have too much respect for her, and you, to ever do something like that. Do you believe me?"

"It happened once, Nick …"

I looked at him under my brow. "I know it did and that was not cool. I know it left a huge distrust for adults in your heart, but have I ever done wrong by you?"

He shook his head and looked like he wanted to believe me.

"No, and I never will. You have my word and you know my word is always truthful."

He nodded just as I spotted Mandy coming toward us. I stood when she came through the door and hugged her, rubbing her back. She was utterly spent and I helped her to a chair.

"How's Esther, Mom?" Ben asked nervously, his sandwich forgotten.

She leaned forward and took his hand. "You did the right thing by calling me. Her wrist is broken and the doctor has to do surgery to fix it. He said if you hadn't been on top of it, and given her the Advil and kept the ice on it, they would have to wait to do surgery, but because you did, they can do it tonight."

Ben's chin trembled and he was fighting back the tears. I put my hand on his shoulder and squeezed it. "It's okay to cry, Ben. This whole thing is terrifying."

Mandy held her arms open and Ben sank into them. "I tried to get Dad to take her, Mom. I really did."

"Shh, it's okay. I know you did and you did everything right. Esther has brittle bones because of her medication, but she will be fine once the surgery is over."

Ben leaned back and wiped his eyes, "Who's with her now?" he asked, staring at the door.

"She fell asleep from the medicine they put in her I.V. to make her arm hurt less. Would you like to sit with her while I talk to Nick and the other doctors?"

Ben nodded and I stood, putting a firm hand on her shoulder. "I'll take him, you need to rest for a moment."

I carried Ben's sandwich and pop while he walked in a trance toward the curtain where Esther was sleeping. I set the food down on a small tray next to her bed and pulled up a chair for him.

I brushed back the hair off Esther's face and was thankful for the peaceful look she wore rather than the pinched, painful one she had earlier. Her arm was held to her chest with a big icepack wrapped around it.

"She looks okay," Ben said, looking to me for confirmation.

"She looks great, and you can be proud that it's all because of you. You did a good job, Ben. We're all proud of you."

He sat in the chair and stuck his hand between the metal bars on the bed, taking her good hand. "I'll stay with her in case she wakes up. Will you take care of my mom? She's tired. I can tell by the way she's walking."

I patted his back twice and nodded once. "I'll go find out what the doctors are going to do and then we'll be back. When I get back here, I want to see your sandwich gone, okay? You need to eat, so you don't need a bed next to Esther's."

He nodded his agreement and I pulled the curtain back and went to the waiting room where Mandy sat, her head back and her eyes closed.

I laid my hand on her shoulder as I went by to let her know I was there. She opened her eyes and smiled at me.

"What a day, huh?" she asked and I chuckled.

"It's always exciting when I'm with you. How are you holding up?"

"I'm okay. Right now, I'm trying not to think about choking the life out of Jacob."

I rubbed her knee and kept my principal face on. "You told Ben that Esther has brittle bones because of her medication. Is she sick?"

She shook her head. "No, well, kind of, but not really."

I raised one brow at her and she laughed, which was music to my ears.

"She's on a proton pump inhibitor for gastric reflux. If she doesn't take it, she gets very ill, but that class of drugs tends to weaken kids' bones. I pump her full of calcium, but this time it wasn't enough."

"She has reflux at eight?" I asked, surprised, and she grimaced.

"She's had it since she was born. My pregnancy with her was difficult. I was working full-time and taking care of Ben the rest of the time since Jacob was never there. I think I already suspected something was going on. The stress of it all put me into early labor. My dad did everything he could, but I delivered Esther a month early. She was perfect and had no problems, other than the reflux. The sphincter in her stomach didn't have time to finish developing and it doesn't work. She has to take the medication, so she doesn't vomit all the time."

I pulled her over next to me on the couch and laid her head on my shoulder. "There's nothing else the doctors can do?"

"There's a surgery they can do to surgically form a sphincter for her. She had to be closer to eight before they did it and the doctor suggested I do it this past summer. It's just that she wanted to go to camp so badly, and it would have taken her the whole summer to recover. After this, though, she's going to have the surgery so she can go off the medication."

I rubbed her shoulder and kissed the top of her head. "Don't beat yourself up. Like I told Ben, kids fall all the time, that's part of being a kid."

"She told me she didn't fall. She was pushed off the skateboard by one of Tasha's kids. She was pretty drugged up, though, so I'm not sure if it's true."

"Ben told me that the other kids are mean to her a lot. He promised not to keep quiet about it this time."

She nodded her head against my shoulder. "I'll talk with them once Esther isn't on drugs that make her goofy."

"I brought Ben some food and he ate like a ravenous wolf. When I asked him when he ate last, he told me it was last night."

She sat back and stared at me with one brow pulled to her nose. "What?"

"I was going to wait to tell you, but I think you should know since Esther told you she was pushed. Ben told me when they go to their grandma's, she feeds them, but when they are with Jacob, it's hit or miss unless Ben cooks something."

She rubbed her temple and shook her head. "I can't let this go on."

I kissed her forehead and kept a firm hand on her knee. "I'll support you any way I can. Let's put that aside for now and focus on Esther. Where is her arm broken and what are they going to do?"

My words helped her focus and she pointed at her wrist. "She broke the bones at the growth plate. That's not a good thing. If it doesn't heal correctly, her right arm could end up being shorter and smaller than her left."

"How small?" I asked, surprised.

"It wouldn't get any bigger than it is now and she's only eight. You know she has a lot of growing to do."

I nodded slowly. "Do the doctors think they can fix it, so that doesn't happen?"

"They will look at her x-rays after the pediatric orthopedic doctor gets here. The doctor I talked to said she's the best in the nation and not to worry."

I held her hand and caressed her face to ease her worry. "We're at Mayo, and if there is any place to be when you have a significant injury, Mayo is the place. She's going to be okay and we'll take her home in a few days."

She glanced up at me. "I'm going to need some time off until she can go back to school. I don't know how I'm going to afford it, though. Maybe my mom can stay with her during the day next week."

I held her chin in my hand. "Mands, I don't want you to worry about this. I already checked and you have twenty-seven sick days. You can use those days to care for a sick child, so take a deep breath and don't worry. Did the doctor say she won't be able to go to school right away?"

"He said it would depend on her pain level. She won't be released until Sunday morning. They will keep her tomorrow to make sure the arm isn't going to swell or cause her excessive pain. He said she will have a soft cast on for a week and won't be able to go to school. After she gets her hard cast on, she can go back."

I smiled encouragingly. "Piece of cake, we can swing a week without you. I know you have the elementary music program to deal with on Wednesday, so if your mom can't stay with her, I'll take the morning off and stay with her, deal?"

She reached up and ran a hand down my face. "You're an incredibly good man, Nick S. Klaus."

I pulled her into a hug and held her tightly. "No, I'm just a man smitten with a woman and her two great kids. I would do anything for you or them. You know that, right?"

She nodded her head against my chest and I kissed her temple. I didn't let her go, leaving her in my arms to gather strength for what was to come. I was more than smitten. I was in love. The best way to tell her that was to show her I was going to be around, even when times were tough. She trembled in my arms and I held her a little tighter, determined to be the one to hold her and give her comfort for the rest of her life.

Chapter Fifteen

We were all gathered in the surgical waiting room, and Mandy was pacing the floor. Ben was curled up on the small couch sleeping since it was well after ten by the time they took Esther back for surgery. The doctor assured us it wouldn't take more than a few hours, but tell that to a very anxious mother. On her way by me for the tenth time, I stood and blocked her way, holding her arms.

"Have you called your family? They need to know what's going on. Maybe they can come and get Ben so he can sleep someplace comfortable. He's worn out, and so are you. He can sleep at their place and they can bring him back tomorrow to see Esther."

She shook her head and rested it on my shoulder. "You know how that's going to go, Nick. Mom will want to come and Dad won't bring her."

I held her by her shoulders and gazed into her eyes. "Mands, this is their granddaughter. They need to know."

"You're right, I just don't have it in me for a fight," she said, defeated.

"Then don't fight. Call and tell them and the

rest will be up to them."

She nodded and pulled her phone out of her pocket, hitting a button. She perched on the edge of a chair and waited.

"Hi, Dad," she said when the phone was answered. "I'm sorry to call so late, but there's been an accident, and Esther broke her arm. She's in surgery here at St. Mary's having it pinned." She rubbed her forehead and listened to the man on the other end of the line.

"We aren't sure exactly what happened. She was playing with the other kids and fell. She broke her wrist through the growth plate, so the doctors felt it was best if we went ahead with surgery to make sure it heals correctly." She paused again and then rolled her eyes.

"They were with their grandparents, Dad. I was at the conference in St. Paul, but Ben called me and I rushed back. He's here sleeping, and I was hoping you could come pick him up? I know it's late, but he's exhausted. He needs a bed and a hot meal in the morning before he comes back to the hospital." She listened for a few moments and her face filled with anger, even as a tear rolled down her cheek. "No, that's fine. I'm sorry to bother you so late. I'll handle it."

I pulled the phone from her hand, my patience with her family gone after a long day. "Sir, this is Nick Klaus," I said into the phone and I heard a sharp intake of breath in my ear.

"Are you with my daughter, Nick?" he asked

suspiciously.

"We rode together to the conference and when Ben called, I drove her back to get Esther."

"I see," he said slowly, and I made a fist with my hand.

"No, I don't think you do see, sir," I spat and Mandy was standing next to me instantly, trying to take the phone. I leaned away so she couldn't. "Your granddaughter, little eight-year-old Esther, is in surgery because your grandson kept his cool and was the only one to give Esther first-aid until we got to them. All your daughter is asking for is a little bit of help with your grandson. I'm likely stepping out of bounds here, but I think it's time you stop using everything that happens as a teachable moment for your daughter. It's time to start being a father and a grandfather. We all make mistakes, Mr. Alexander, and I think we both know that Mandy has paid very heavily for hers. Your blatant disrespect veiled as tough love is simply unacceptable. Being a father means being there to support your child, even when you disagree with their choices. Now, if you'll excuse me, I need to tend to your daughter who is near collapse. We will keep you updated by text as to the condition of your granddaughter, but we won't bother you again otherwise."

I didn't give him a chance to respond, simply hit the end button and dropped my hand to my side, sucking in air through my nostrils. I glanced at Mandy and tears were rolling down her cheeks as she stood there, swaying from exhaustion.

"My God, Nick, what did you just do?" she moaned.

I grabbed her before she fell and sat her down in a chair. I knelt in front of her, pushing her hair back away from her face and holding her eyes.

"I did what needed to be done, and it needed to be done by someone not afraid of changing their relationship with him. I like your dad, I really do. I've worked with him for years with the Coats for Kids program, but I can't stand by and let him continue to treat you this way. Ben knows his grandpa treats him differently than he treats Dully's and Jake's kids. It's time for this to end, but the ball is in his court now."

"And that's where it's going to stay. He's too stubborn to hit it back. I'm just too tired to worry about it right now."

"Okay, then sit here quietly with me while we wait for the doctor to finish. Ben is comfortable for now and once we know Esther is okay, I'll take him home. He can sleep at my place then I'll bring him back in the morning. Okay?"

She leaned her head back on the chair and nodded, her eyes going closed and her body relaxing just a hair.

I closed my eyes and prayed I didn't screw everything up by telling Tom Alexander exactly like it is. People in Snowberry think the sun rises and sets with him, and it's time for him to step up and be the person everyone believes him to be.

Something told me he would, I just wondered how long it would take him to do it and if it would be too late.

"Mrs. Alexander?"

Mandy looked up from the email she was typing when she heard the doctor's voice.

"Yes, Dr. Howell. How is Esther?" she asked quickly.

The doctor sat across from Mandy and laid a hand on her knee. "Call me Janet, please. Dr. Howell makes me feel like a middle-aged man."

Mandy chuckled and nodded. "Of course, Janet. Are you done already? It's only been an hour."

"Things went textbook perfect, actually. She had a clean break and your son really did her a favor by immediately stopping the soft tissue swelling. She's going to be just fine."

Mandy visibly relaxed with Janet's words. "Thank God. Do you think her arm will be the same length as the other?"

Janet nodded. "I'm not worried about that after seeing how well it went back together. Growth plate breaks can be tricky, but this one was clean through, no jagged edges, and I was able to repair it with only two screws. The screws will absorb into the bone and we won't have to remove them as we've had to in the past."

I sat forward. "Those were developed at the Fraunhofer Institute, right?"

Janet turned to me and raised one brow, which nearly touched the top of her surgical cap. "They were, as a matter of fact."

I chuckled at the look on her face. "Sorry, I was born and raised in Germany. I didn't mean to interrupt."

She laughed easily. "No apology necessary. There isn't much more to say. I think we will be able to release her later tomorrow afternoon," she said, checking her watch. "She's in a soft cast and we will need to see her next Friday to get that changed. I'll be in around two tomorrow afternoon to check on her. I'll lay out the treatment plan with you before she's discharged."

Mandy sat forward. "I thought you had to keep her until Sunday."

"That's usually what happens after this kind of surgery, but with the early intervention she got, and the clean break, I don't foresee any swelling issues. Of course, I've been wrong before, so I'll make that decision when I come in to check on her later."

Mandy nodded. "Okay, thank you, Janet. I appreciate you coming in tonight to take care of her."

Janet patted Mandy's hand and smiled. "That's my job. Kids shouldn't be in pain just so an adult can get their beauty rest." She winked and stood. "The plastic surgeon is suturing her wound as we speak. I asked him to come in and perform the closure. I know girls don't want scars where everyone can see them. He will take his time and make sure that when she heals, you won't see anything. Once he's done, she will go to recovery and the nurse will come get you. Then you can stay with her until they move her to a room." She walked to where Ben was asleep, oblivious to what was going on around him.

Janet picked up his hand and gave it a squeeze. "You did a good job, big brother," she whispered to the sleeping boy, then waved to us and left the room.

Mandy hung her head, tears falling from her eyes. "I'm so relieved."

I pulled her up and into my arms, holding her tightly. "Me, too. She's going to wake up and be just fine. She's a fighter, just like her mom."

"Mandy!" A shrill voice called out and we both turned to see Suzie hurrying through the waiting area. She threw her arms around Mandy and I held them both, so Mandy didn't tip over. "How's my baby girl?"

Mandy held her mom and I could tell by the look on her face how much it meant to her that she came. "She's okay, Mom. The doctor just left and said everything went perfectly. She's in recovery and they will come to get me soon to go see her. Dr. Howell thinks she might be able to go home late tomorrow afternoon."

"We got here as fast as we could after you

called. Why didn't you call earlier?" she asked, leaning back to hold her daughter's face.

"I didn't think about it. I'm sorry. I was so worried about Esther, I wasn't thinking about anything else."

"Oh, how I know that feeling," she whispered, smiling at her daughter. "I'm glad you called. We will stay until we can see Esther and then we'll take Ben with us so he can sleep. We'll bring him back tomorrow or keep him until Esther is released, whatever you would like."

"Okay, thanks, Mom. You said we …" Mandy said and then froze when her dad walked toward us.

"Dad was parking the car," Suzie explained.

Tom walked up to Mandy and pulled her into a hug, holding her so tight I was afraid she couldn't breathe. "I'm sorry, Mandy," he whispered. "Can you ever forgive me?"

Mandy held him just as tightly. "We need to talk, Dad, but right now, I'm worried about Esther."

He loosened his grip and nodded, patting her face as if he was seeing the little girl he used to know. "I'm sorry I wasn't here more for you and the kids. That's over now. That's my solemn vow to you tonight. We can talk another time, but I want you to promise me that you won't hesitate to ask for help ever again."

Mandy nodded and Tom hugged her again before turning to look at Ben on the couch. "He looks so big. When did he grow up?"

"He's a good boy," Mandy said, her eyes lit up with pride as she gazed at him. "He's the reason Esther was able to have surgery tonight instead of having to suffer in pain until the swelling went down. He did what the adults at that place wouldn't do, and that was to use common sense. He kept her arm elevated, used ice, and gave her Advil to control the swelling. He's eleven, Dad. He shouldn't have to be the man in that house."

Tom knelt down next to Ben and shook his head. "No, he shouldn't, but God love him for looking after his sister."

"I'm too tired to think right now, but once I can, I know what I have to do. I have to petition the court to change the mandatory visitation rights. They aren't safe there and this was the final straw for me. I'll tell you and Mom about it once I talk to my lawyer. I need to know how much it's going to cost, so I can save money and start the proceedings. I want Jacob out of their lives, even if that means I lose my child support. That man is no father."

Tom stood back up and took Suzie's hand. "Your mom and I are behind you one hundred percent. Whatever you need, say the word and it's done. I'll pay Kate's fees and anything else that comes up. You all need a fresh start and that's money well spent as far as I'm concerned."

Mandy kept her head high and nodded. "I'll come over and talk with you once I've seen Kate. It will be a few weeks, but I'm going to ask her to file a temporary custody break until Esther has healed. She won't be going back there in the condition she's in."

I held Mandy's waist and pointed toward a nurse approaching us. The nurse stopped and matched the band on Mandy's wrist to the chart in her hand and then smiled. "Ms. Alexander, your daughter is starting to wake up, and we thought you might like to be there with her."

"Yes, yes, I would," Mandy said quickly, glancing between her parents and me.

Tom bent and scooped up Ben, who startled awake in his arms. "You're okay, Ben. It's me, Grandpa Tom. Grandma and I are going to take you to a hotel to sleep, so you can stay close to Mom and Esther, okay?"

Ben rubbed his eyes. "How is Esther? I want to see her," he said with his head hanging over his grandpa's shoulder.

I went behind Tom's back so Ben could see me. "She's just waking up from surgery, but the doctor said it went perfectly. You go with your grandparents now and sleep. They'll bring you over in the morning to see her once she's had time to sleep, too, okay, bud?"

He nodded and his eyes closed again. It made me wonder how much sleep he got at his dad's when they were there.

I patted Tom on the shoulder. "Thanks for taking him. I'll stay with Mandy and Esther and keep you updated by text."

My eyes fell on Suzie, who was hugging her daughter with tears in her eyes, but a smile on her face. The nurse waited patiently in the corner for us and I put my hand on Mandy's back.

"The nurse is waiting, love," I said softly.

Suzie stepped away from Mandy and gave me a quick hug, too. "Thanks for being here, Nick. I know our family can be a lot to deal with sometimes. I appreciate everything you've done to help tonight."

"It's no problem, Mrs. Alexander," I assured her, and she stepped back and picked up her purse.

"Just call me Suzie, Nick. We'll be at the hotel across the street. We brought him a change of clothes and I'll make sure he gets a shower and breakfast in the morning. I'll text Mandy the room number in case you need anything."

They left with a tired boy and I put my arm around Mandy's waist and guided her toward the nurse who led us to the recovery room. "Looks like he hit it back."

She glanced up at me and I winked, which made her smile.

Chapter Sixteen

"I'm hungry, mommy," Esther said from the backseat as I drove into Snowberry proper.

Mandy turned in her seat to see her little girl. "What are you hungry for, baby? I think I need to get some groceries."

"I want pie," Ben piped up and I snickered while I drove.

"I want pie, too," I said to egg him on.

"I want pie. How about some of Aunt Liberty's pecan pie? I think that would make my arm feel much better," Esther said.

"I don't have any of Aunt Liberty's pie and the bakery is already closed. Maybe tomorrow we could get pie?" she asked, the fatigue in her voice obvious.

I pulled the car up to the curb and turned off the engine. The light was starting to wane at four in the afternoon, but it was Saturday, and Kiss's Café was open late.

"How about if we let someone else do the cooking?" I asked. "Dinner is on me, you can have anything you want, and pie."

Mandy turned in her seat and saw the restaurant through the window. She sagged a little in her seat. "Sounds perfect. Esther, let me help you out, so you don't hurt your arm."

I climbed out of the driver's side and went around to the back, opening her door.

Esther looked up at us. "I want Nick to carry me."

Mandy gave half a snort, while I reached in and pulled the girl out carefully. She rested on my hip and kept her right arm tight to her side in the sling. They had it pulled up until it was under her chin and nearly vertical against her chest, to keep the swelling down.

Ben climbed out of the car and we all trudged into the almost empty café.

"Mandy? What happened?" Savannah exclaimed when she saw Esther. Savannah owns the café with her husband Noel and like me, she had a little one attached to her hip.

I reached my hand out and tickled the baby's fingers. "Hello, Luke, you're looking handsome tonight."

The baby tucked his face into his mom's neck and dug his toes into her belly to hide from me. Savannah rubbed his back while she frowned.

"We just got back from having dinner at church. I wondered why I didn't see any of your family there, Mandy. What happened?"

She patted Esther on the back and led us to a booth so I could sit with her on my lap.

Mandy let Ben climb in first and then sat. She

pointed at Esther. "She fell at her grandma's house before her dad's wedding. Her wrist broke and she had surgery last night at St. Mary's. They released her a bit ago and we just got back to town. Everyone was hungry, so you know where we go when we need comfort food."

Savannah frowned deeper. "Oh, poor Esther, I'm so sorry you fell. I'll make sure Millie makes your pancakes just the way you like them, with extra chocolate chips."

Savannah disappeared with Luke to get a waitress and Esther held her elbow. "Mommy, I didn't fall, I was pushed. You shouldn't lie to people."

Mandy glanced up from the menu and leaned over the table. "I know, baby, but sometimes there are things that should stay between us. You fell because you were pushed, but I'm leaving that out because it's private between us, okay?"

Esther seemed happy with the explanation and laid back on my chest, her body heavy with fatigue. "I want pancakes and pie," she whispered as her eyes went closed.

Mandy smiled at the little girl and then helped Ben decide what he wanted. When the waitress came back to the table, she took our order quietly and then tucked the menus under her arm and put the order in.

"Sam?" Ben asked and his mom looked confused.

I chuckled. "He's trying to guess what the S stands for in my middle name."

She looked at Ben and then at me. "What does it stand for?"

"I'll never tell, but I did promise Ben if he guessed it, I would tell him the truth. No, it's not Sam."

Ben screwed his mouth up and then lifted his eyebrows. "Selig?" I shook my head and snorted. "Sigfrid? Sherman?"

"Double negative." I winked and he frowned until the waitress showed up with our drinks.

Mandy poured coffee in her cup and drank the cup almost in one swallow then refilled it. I laid my hand on her arm. "Slow down, it's late and you don't want to be awake all night."

She looked up at me as though she wasn't even thinking, just going through the motions. "I still have to get groceries when we're done here. Can you stay with the kids while I run to the store? I emptied the fridge, thinking I would have time before they got home to get groceries."

"I'm happy to stay with them, but groceries are taken care of. I have a sub covering your classes for the rest of the week, and postponed the elementary program until next Thursday."

"Nick!" she exclaimed quietly. "How is that going to look?"

Ben put his arm around his mom and looked concerned. "What's the matter, Mom? Esther got hurt and she needs you. You're not going to look bad. Besides, Esther won't want to miss the program at the old folks' home."

I pointed at Ben. "Right, what he said. I sent out a district-wide phone call. I'm surprised you didn't get the call."

"My phone is dead, remember?" she hissed and I chuckled at her. She crossed her arms over her chest and stuck out her chin. "And it's the retirement village, Ben, not the old folks' home. Who took care of the groceries?"

"December and Liberty," I answered. "Your mom said they wanted to help, so I sent them on errands to make the house comfortable for the next week. I'll take Ben to school with me and bring him home at the end of the day. If you want, I'll take Friday off and drive you to Rochester, or you can go yourself. Whichever feels right at the time."

She threw her arms out and almost decked Ben in the nose. "So, you're just going to waltz in and take over my life now? I've been their mother for the last eleven years. I can do this!"

She wasn't quiet and Esther woke in my arms, her eyes wide as she stared at her mom. I settled her on the booth next to me and held my hands out to Mandy. "I know you can, Mandy. I was only trying to help."

"You aren't being very nice, Mom," Ben scolded. "Nick is making it easier on you for the next week. Why are you mad?"

She dropped her arms and pushed herself out of the booth, speed walking away from the table.

I pointed at Ben. "Stay here, I'll be right back."

He nodded and I took off for the back of the café, or rather the front by all rights, where I saw her disappear.

Savannah pointed at the long hallway as I passed her. "I'll stay with the kids," she promised and I gave her a thankful smile.

I pushed through the door to see Mandy leaning against the rail, sobbing.

"Mandy, it's okay," I promised, remembering to warn her before I put my arms around her. She cried harder and I held her, my arms wrapped around her while her tears fell on my arms. "Shh, Ben shouldn't have said that, but he's just a kid."

She turned in my arms and buried her face in my shirt. "I'm sorr-rry," she hiccupped. "I'm tired and worried. I think I'm hav-ving a delayed re-action to everything that's happened."

I kissed her temple and tried to comfort her. "I know. You didn't get much sleep last night and now the reality of everything is hitting you. You need a hot meal, a hot shower, and a good sleep in your own bed. Tomorrow things will be easier to deal with. I promise."

She nodded and I helped her calm down by holding her and rubbing her back. When she was quiet, I spoke again. "I'm sorry for overstepping my bounds, but I wanted to make it a little easier for you. I wasn't trying to make you feel like you can't do this alone. I've watched you do it alone for the last five years and I have no doubt you still can, but it doesn't make you look weak to accept help once in a while."

She leaned back against the rail and wiped her face with the napkin I had taken from Savannah's hand when I went by. "I have this awful fear in my stomach about what's going to happen when Jacob finds out I'm not letting the kids be there anymore."

I tipped her chin up. "Hey, you don't have to face that alone, either. Besides, you're putting the cart before the horse. Talk to the lawyer and outline a plan first."

"I know. I hate feeling like this."

"How are you feeling?" I asked, hoping she could explain it better.

Her chin started to tremble. "Like I've failed. I thought I was doing everything right, but now I can see that I really wasn't. I didn't want to make waves, so I let my kids see me being passive about my father all these years. No wonder Ben kept going to Jacob's even though he knew it wasn't safe. I. Taught. Him. That," she cried, jabbing herself in the chest.

I grabbed her and wrapped my arms around her tight, laying my lips next to her ear. "Mandy, honey, stop. This didn't happen because of the way Tom has treated you in the past years. Maybe your dad took too harsh of a line with you, but if you were hurt or in danger, he would never hesitate to help you. Ben knows that. He kept going to Jacob's because he wanted some kind of relationship with him, even if it wasn't ideal. No one likes to give up on their dad."

"Even when their dad has given up on them?" she asked, her voice soft in the night.

"I don't think Ben had come to that conclusion yet. He has now, but he was trying to be a good person. Now that he's seen who Jacob really is, and how little he cares, he told me he doesn't feel guilty anymore. He said he tried, but he can't fix the broken morals of a man three times his age."

She hung her head over the edge of the railing suddenly and I grabbed her waist, steadying her. I couldn't decide what she was doing, so I rubbed her back until she settled again. "Are you okay?"

She rested her head on her hand, her elbow propped on the handrail. "I thought I was going to vomit hearing you say those words. I can't believe he told you that. I feel so horrible right now," she whispered.

I turned her around to face me and held her face in my hands. "I know I'm not a parent, Mandy, but I like to think I have enough experience with kids to be able to read their real feelings when they talk to me. When he said those things to me, he wasn't angry or spiteful. He said the words, but he knows that he can't change his father, and he knows, no matter what, you love him enough for two parents. He's forgiven Jacob, even though he doesn't want anything more to do with him. You need to spend some time with him and talk this out, but he doesn't want you to blame yourself. He's so proud of who you are. Hang on to that and let the rest go."

She nodded her head, still in my hands. "Are the kids okay?" she asked, suddenly aware they weren't with me.

"They're fine. Savannah was letting them play with Luke. I'm sure our food is probably ready, so we should go back in." I leaned down and kissed her lips before leading her back to the door. I followed her down the hall and the kids were sitting quietly at the table, staring at their plates of steaming food.

When Ben saw us, he scooted out of the booth and grabbed his mom around the waist. "I'm sorry. I shouldn't have been disrespectful."

She ruffled his hair and hugged him for a moment before encouraging him to slide back into the booth.

"I'm sorry for getting upset. Mom's just really, really tired and scared."

Esther looked at me as I cut her pancakes for her. "Mom's scared because of me, isn't she? I didn't mean for this to happen."

I dropped the fork and hugged her little head to my chest while Mandy took her good hand. "No, baby, it's not your fault, it's Devon's fault. I know you don't want to be sitting there in pain any more than I want to see you in pain, but what's done is done. We're all tired, that's all. We need to eat our food and go home for a good night's sleep. Nick promises that in the morning, everything will be better."

Esther stared up at me and I nodded. "It will be, and pretty soon it will be Friday and you'll have a cool new cast. Then you'll be ready to go back to school."

She seemed happy with that answer, so she picked up her fork and stabbed a piece of the pancake while Ben pushed his fries around his plate.

"Ben, it's okay, no one is upset with you," Mandy said again. He finally relented and picked up his burger, taking a bite.

I reached my hand across the booth and took Mandy's hand. "Maybe it's okay if Ben stays home tomorrow, too. He might need to sleep in."

"I'll be fine, Nick," he said, "I don't want to miss school on a Monday. Mrs. Sweet picks reading books for the week and if you aren't there, you don't get a say in the matter." He shuddered and shook his head. "She'll have me reading Twilight or something."

Mandy laughed and I covered my mouth with my hand. "We don't want that. I'll pick you up at eight and go in a little late. That way, you can sleep as long as possible in the morning."

Ben nodded and went back to his plate, but Esther stared up at me and frowned. "I want you to stay at my house with me, Nick. If you stay, then Mommy can sleep, and if I need water, you can get it for me."

Mandy laughed a little and shook her head. "Esther, honey, Nick has to work tomorrow. He needs to get some sleep, too."

"But we have a couch," she said logically and I bit my tongue to keep from laughing.

"I'll tell you what, little lady. After we eat and get everyone settled at home, we can talk about it. Deal?"

"Deal," she answered, bobbing her head once. "Now, would someone please help me stab these pancakes? Using my left hand is going to take some getting used to."

We all laughed and I picked up her fork, popping a piece in her mouth.

Chapter Seventeen

I hung up the phone and took a drink of my gin and tonic. It was Saturday and I wasn't supposed to be working, but I had been putting out fires all day at school. The latest problem was a broken lock on the front door. The janitor assured me that nothing had been stolen because the interior doors hadn't been breached, but I asked the police to send an officer to make an official report anyway. We would have to pay for the broken lock if it wasn't vandalism, and they could tell me the fastest.

What a long two weeks it had been since MEA. Things had finally settled down again for Mandy, but we hadn't been alone together since. I spent most evenings at her house now that Esther was back at school. I hoped to convince her to watch a movie with me tonight once the kids were in bed. It was nearly four and I hadn't heard from her all day. I was trying not to be overbearing, but I wanted to text her every few minutes to see if she was okay. So far, I had resisted, but that doesn't mean I haven't looked out my window multiple times for her.

I stood and stretched my back, heading for the

door to not so subtly look to see if her lights were on again when there was a knock on the door. I pulled it open to her beautiful face and relief flowed through me.

I pulled her in the door and closed it, pressing her up against it and laying my lips against hers, taking what I needed. Her hands came up and wound into my hair, holding my head to her lips and whimpering as though it had been years since we were last together. She slowly came back to earth and she stiffened against me. I pulled back and kissed her neck a few times, then took a good look at her.

"What's the matter?" I asked, taking in her darkened eyes and red cheeks, and knew it wasn't from the kiss.

"It's been a really long day," she said, pushing off the door.

I held my hand out and she took it. "Where are the kids?"

"They're at the Liberty Belle making Halloween cookies for the community center party tomorrow. Then they're having a sleepover at my mom and dad's. Tomorrow is Halloween, you know."

I groaned. "Oh, I know. I love it when the kids are all hyped up the day after Halloween at school. It always makes for a great Monday." I rolled my eyes and she laughed, nodding.

"I have to meet them for Sunday dinner and then take them to the party at two. Do you want to come?"

"Yeah, I want to come. Am I really invited?"

"I wouldn't have asked if you weren't."

I led her into the living room and pointed to the couch. "Sit. Can I get you some pop?"

She waved her hand. "Do you have anything stronger?"

I raised a brow and went to the bar, pulling out Captain Morgan and holding it up. She nodded and I poured a generous helping in and added Coke to the top. She took it and drank it down in one swallow. She lowered the glass and the ice clanked in the bottom, then she held it out to me. "Fill 'er up, Sam."

I took the glass and repeated my earlier routine, chuckling when she belched like a sailor from the carbonation. When I turned back, she had her hand over her mouth.

I handed her the glass. "This is not a belch-free zone. Feel free to let it all out."

She sipped the second drink slower and leaned back in the chair. "I just got back from my lawyer's."

I sat, folding my hands on my lap. "On a Saturday?"

"Kate is a family friend and was gathering information up until this point. She called me today to come in and discuss it."

"What does *gathering information* mean?"

"Phone records, emails, talking to the right people, that kind of thing."

"I'm confused. Why would she need to do that?"

"You know this was supposed to be Jacob's weekend to have the kids, but I agreed months ago to keep them home since he would be newly married?" I nodded agreement. "Well, since the day we picked Esther and Ben up from his house, I haven't heard from him."

"At all? Not a call or a text?"

She shook her head. "Nothing, and he said they weren't going on a honeymoon, so we thought he was in town. He never even called to check on his daughter. Can you believe that?"

"Honestly, no, I can't, but then yes, I can. Only because I've seen a lot of things in my days as a principal. He was rather ... angry about me being there that day. He asked me if I was your newest booty call."

She shook her head and took a long drink of the alcohol. "As if I've ever had a booty call before. What a piece of work."

"I told him to shove it, if that matters to you." She smiled behind the glass and I gave myself two points for that. "What did your lawyer say when you told him he refused to get her treatment and hasn't called or checked on her?"

"She's a family and divorce lawyer, Nick. She wasn't surprised, but she was angry. She never liked Jacob, but she likes him even less now."

"What did she find?" I asked slowly, taking the drink from her hand.

"It's more like what she didn't find. Kate was looking for any communication that he had made an effort to contact me, which of course, we know he didn't. What she found instead was that he stopped his direct deposit, so the government couldn't take his child support, and he tried to disappear."

"You're kidding me, right?"

She shook her head and took the drink from my hand, slamming it back. She smacked her lips and set the glass on the table. "No, he packed up Tasha and her kids, quit paying rent, and quit his job. Apparently, he moved to California, where there was a mission position waiting."

"He can't do that. It's not legal."

She laughed and rolled her eyes at me. "He can do anything he wants, Nick, even if it is illegal. Kate's detective tracked Jacob down easily and we called him this afternoon."

I was off the chair and kneeling in front of her. "What happened?" I asked, running my finger over the puffiness of her cheeks.

"He doesn't want anything to do with our children. He said as far as he's concerned, he's not even sure they are his."

"What?" I exclaimed a little too loudly. I brought my voice down and took her hands. "Why would he say that?"

"I don't know, Nick. It's like he wants to pretend we don't exist."

"What did you tell him?" I asked, trying to keep

my anger in check.

"I pointed out that it was him who cheated and not me, and then my lawyer reminded him we had paternity on him from the divorce."

"Has he said before they aren't his?"

She rubbed her leg nervously. "Yeah, when we first split up, he claimed they couldn't be his because he was sterile." She laughed. "What a joke. I had the DNA tests done to prove paternity. He didn't have a leg to stand on after that. For the first two years after the divorce, he only saw the kids once or twice a year, but when they got older, he wanted them more often as the custody agreement ordered. My hands were tied, so I let them go. I always knew something was going to happen to one of the kids. The thing is, I couldn't prove it to the court."

"Can you prove it now?" I asked, and she nodded.

"I can, but it doesn't matter. Once we reminded him that they are his and he has legal obligations to them, he was begging me to let him sign away his rights."

I sat back on my butt as if I'd been pushed. "You've got to be kidding me."

She grimaced. "I wish I was. My poor kids. What terrible mistakes I've made."

I took her hands and looked her in the eye. "Remember, getting married is the reason why you have them. The only one who made mistakes here is Jacob. You've done everything right since those kids were born."

"I should never have married him, but …"

"As I told Ben not too long ago, shoulda, coulda, and woulda are useless words because they are past tense. You can't change them, so stay in the present and look to the future."

She thought about that for a few moments and finally smiled. "I never looked at it that way, but you're right. I'm doing now what I should have done then and banishing him from my life."

"You're going to let him sign away his rights? You'll lose child support."

She threw up her hands. "What else can I do, Nick? He's not going to pay it anyway and all I can do is put him in jail, but for what? My kids already know their father doesn't love them. Why drag it out? He asked my lawyer to draw up the paperwork for him to sign and send it to a lawyer in California. He wants out of our lives and the little bit of money I occasionally get from him isn't worth the heartache. Especially when he doesn't want any part of them. If I have to, I'll sell the house and move into something smaller. Maybe I should anyway, that house is nothing but memories of him. Maybe we just need a clean break."

I hugged her and picked her up, settling her on my lap on the couch. "Do you use the money he sends right now for the kids, or do you save it?"

"I save it for the extra things they need like camp. I can more than cover our day-to-day expenses from my checks. I didn't think it was smart to count on his money as part of my budget every month and now I'm glad I didn't. I'll take a second job if I have to in order to cover extra expenses that come up, but my kids won't suffer."

I smoothed back her hair and kissed her forehead. "I had no doubt that would be the case. I'll help any way I can, Mandy."

She glanced down and fingered the buttons on my shirt. "I might not be able to pay you back for the legs until I sell the house, but I will pay you back. I'm going to have added expenses with Esther's surgery now."

I took her hand and kissed it. "Will you do me a favor?" She nodded and I held my finger under her chin so she couldn't look down. "Don't make any decisions until spring. It's going to be too hard to sell the house and move right now. Once spring rolls around, you'll have a better idea if he's really going to sign the paperwork or not. I'm not worried about the money for the legs, and I'm going to cover the bills for Esther's surgery, too."

She shook her head. "No, you can't do that."

"Why can't I? I have so much money sitting there and nothing to spend it on."

"You just can't, and why would you want to?" she asked, tears filling her voice.

"Because I love you, and I love your kids, Mands. I love you, and I want to take some of the burdens off your shoulders, so you can smile again," I whispered, watching her eyes close and her windpipe bob up and down when she swallowed.

"You love us?" she squeaked.

I brushed a kiss across her knuckles. "Yes, I love you. I've known for a long time, but I didn't want to say it and scare you. I think you need to hear it now, so you know you aren't alone."

"You love us?"

I ran one finger down her cheek and tapped her nose, chuckling. "Yes, I love you so much that sometimes it hurts. I also love Ben and Esther. Is this really so surprising to you?"

She shook her head. "Ben asked me last week if I love you."

"He did, did he? What did you say?"

"I told him the truth. I love you, but I made him promise not to tell you."

My heart was in my throat, but I swallowed it down and kissed her cheek. "That's good enough for me, for now."

She took my face in her hands and brought her lips to mine. She kissed me tenderly, in a way she had never kissed me before.

"I love you, Nick. You make my life so much more wonderful by being you and being here for us. I don't want to think about going back to the way it was."

I kissed her sweet lips and whispered, "Then don't think about it. I'm not going anywhere."

She caught my hand and brought it to her breast. "Make love to me, please."

I stood up in one motion and carried her to

my bed, laying her across the soft comforter. "I thought you'd never ask."

Chapter Eighteen

I leaned against the wall, watching Ben and Esther bob for apples. The afternoon of fun was a welcome relief from the uncomfortable few hours I spent with her family for Sunday dinner. It felt like a cross between the Spanish inquisition and Family Feud. I ended up spending more time with Ben, Jay, and Dully playing basketball than I did with Mandy. She assured me it was fine and she understood, but I promised to make it up to her later and make it up I would.

Last night had been a welcome relief after not holding her for two weeks, but with Jacob not taking the kids anymore, it would be hard to carve out that time for only us. I promised her we would, even if I had to pay a sitter to stay with the kids while she came to my house for some much needed R&R. She had laughed and said, "Sure, no one will know we are over here under the sheets if I walk next door." I told her all she had to do was drive around the block and walk through the alley. No one would be the wiser.

I laughed as Ben came up from the bucket with a big red apple in his mouth and his hands in the air. He was dressed as Iron Man and had his mask pushed to the top of his head. Esther decided to use her cast to her advantage and dressed like a zombie patient. She pulled it off well, too.

"Some party they got going here," a voice said, handing me a cold glass of punch.

I raised it to him and took a drink. "Thanks, Mr. Alexander. Holding up the wall is thirsty work."

"But that's not what you're doing, is it?" he asked.

I bounced on my heels a few times. "No, I'm looking after Esther for Mandy while she gets ready to play her spooktacular concert for the kids."

"Why?"

"Why what?" I asked, confused.

"Why are you looking after Esther?" He copied my posture and waited for me to answer. I hadn't had a chance to talk with him at dinner today. He barely made it back from delivering a baby in time for the last of the pot roast. Apparently, he was making up for lost time now.

"I don't want her to fall and get hurt, but I also don't want her to miss the fun. I happened to see Xander prowling around here, too. I need to make sure he doesn't do something stupid and hurt her arm."

"Are you acting purely in principal capacity?"

I groaned inwardly, unsure of how to respond, so I decided honesty was best.

"What are you really asking here, Tom? What

my intentions are? I intend to take care of Mandy and her kids. I love your daughter and I love her kids. It's not exactly rocket science."

He cocked one side of his lip into a smile and took a drink. "Well, that's the most honest any of my children's dates have ever been with me. I admire that. You've got guts, Nick, no doubt about that."

"It doesn't take guts to be there for the woman I love, Tom."

He paused for a moment before responding, as though the words I said were somehow connected to the way he was feeling.

"No, I suppose it comes pretty easily. It should have been me who was there for her these past years, and it took one furious principal to make me see that. I've apologized to Mandy, but I owe you one as well."

I shook my head. "No, you really don't. You haven't said nor done anything to me that was out of line. I simply couldn't stand to watch that beautiful woman feel inferior to her own family any longer. I should be the one apologizing for being disrespectful, but at the time, I felt it was necessary to put the two of you on the right track."

"And you were right. She came over yesterday after she saw the lawyer. Did she tell you?"

"She told me she saw the lawyer, but not that she talked to you."

"Her mother and I will make sure the lawyer gets paid, so she won't have the added expense.

Jacob has cost her enough already. I'm happy to pay the small fortune it will cost for him to be out of our lives for good. Esther and Ben deserve more than what Jacob can offer, and this is a good way to boost their self-worth."

"I don't follow, sir. It might do just the opposite if they know their father didn't care about them enough to even be on their birth certificates."

"Kids know more than we think they do. Ben told me Jacob was only taking them so Tasha's kids had someone to play with. If Ben was there, then Jacob and Tasha got alone time because he would babysit the other three. He knew he was being used."

I grimaced. "I knew Ben had issues with him, but he didn't tell me that."

"No, I suppose he wouldn't. You're a mandatory reporter and his mom is, too."

"I think in the long run, they will be happier just the three of them. Jacob caused a level of stress there that none of them needed. Not to mention, look what happened to Esther."

Tom searched the room until he found Mandy. Without turning his head, he pointed at her feet. "She told me you paid for her new prostheses."

"Only the co-pay," I clarified.

"Why did you do that?"

I let the empty glass of punch hang at my side. "She needed them and she was in pain. Making her wait until she could afford them wasn't something I was willing to do. She's paid for the last two sets alone, Tom."

He nodded slightly. "She told me. I'll pay you back whatever it cost with gratitude for doing what I should have done."

"Not necessary, Tom. There were no strings attached and I didn't expect to be repaid. I would prefer you help Mandy the next few months if she needs it. She will be losing her child support, and she's a little worried about extra expenses that come up like camp for the kids. I plan to pay Esther's hospital bills to help take care of that expense."

He nodded, his eyes watching his granddaughter try to get an apple while keeping her cast dry. "I'm happy to be rid of Jacob. He caused so much pain for our family, not that I helped matters, but not taking his own child to the hospital is a whole new low, even for him. The things you said to me that night were the things I've been saying to myself for a long, long time. Hearing them from an outsider to the family was tough. I heard in your words what I already knew. I had to change. I held Ben in the hotel room the whole night because I wanted to get back all the years I'd wasted."

"Mandy knew you loved her. Don't beat yourself up. Sometimes circumstances beyond our control end up taking control of our lives. I wanted to give her the control back, so she could put Jacob behind her and move on."

"With you?" he asked, finally turning to me.

"God willing, but I only have honest intentions,

sir."

We both heard the music start at the same time and glanced up to see Mandy at the piano and all the kids rushing toward her.

Without looking at me, he pushed off the wall. "I sure hope so, Nick. I like you, and I think you're good for Mandy and the kids, but if you hurt her the way Jacob did, I'll kill you."

"Understood."

He walked away without looking back and I smiled, relief flooding my gut. *Nice talk, Mr. Alexander*, I chuckled to myself. I put half a smile on my face and joined the kids by the piano.

My phone was chirping at me when I climbed out of the shower after my jog. It was Saturday morning and I really didn't want to deal with school again. I dried off and grabbed the phone, opening the text. It was Ben texting me from his iPad.

"Nick, mom keeps crying and won't tell us why. Can you come over?"

"I'll be right there."

I grabbed my pants off the bed and stepped into them, then tossed my shirt over my head on the way to the front door for my shoes. In the past two weeks since Halloween, Ben and I had spent a lot of time together after school. Sometimes we played basketball in the school gym while his mom was practicing with the soloists for the Christmas concert, and sometimes I brought him and Esther home for a snack and homework help. Esther had begged me to teach her some German, so we had fun learning animal names this week.

Mandy was stressed out with the upcoming Christmas concert in a month, but it was nothing to cry about. Something else must have happened. I let myself in through the patio doors and found Ben pacing in the kitchen while Esther colored at the table.

I put my hand on his shoulder and knelt next to him. "What happened to make her cry?"

He held out his palms. "I really don't know. She keeps going to the bathroom and I know it's so she can cry without us seeing her."

I stood and led him to the table to sit with Esther. "I'll be right back."

I headed down the hallway toward her room just as she came out of the bathroom. Her eyes were red-rimmed and her cheeks puffy, but her face was dry. I held my arms out and she walked into them. I closed mine around her and walked slowly toward her room, pushing the door shut.

"What's the matter, Mands? Ben said you've been crying this morning."

"Ben doesn't understand that moms cry sometimes."

"That's true, but usually, they have a reason."

She patted my chest as though I was a small child and she didn't want to explain herself to me. "I'm a little overwhelmed with work and home. I know they want to do something fun today, but I have so much to do."

I looked her in the eye and knew that was a crock of kraut, as my dad used to say. There was way more to it than that, but maybe a little time alone would help her sort it out.

"Why don't you let me take the kids out for the day and you can get caught up on your work?"

She glanced up and her face looked torn between agreeing and objecting. "I can't ask you to do that, Nick."

"You can, but you didn't, I offered. I love spending time with Ben and Esther. Let me take them for a few hours and then we'll all have dinner together tonight, okay?"

"I appreciate it like you don't know," she whispered.

I bent down and kissed her gently. "Would you like me to get you a coffee first?"

"No, I'll make some here and drink it while I work."

I kissed her hand and then let it fall, walking back down the hall to the kitchen. There were two anxious faces staring at me and I motioned to them. "Huddle up, guys, we gotta make a game plan."

"This was a pretty good game plan, Nick," Esther clapped excitedly when they brought her pop to the table at Gallo's.

I huffed on my fingers and rubbed them on my chest. "I thought so. Did you have fun?"

"It was great to see my friends at the roller rink," Ben agreed.

"I liked that you could carry me and skate, Nick. This darn thing has got to go," she grumped, shaking her casted arm.

"Yeah, I didn't know you could skate like that," Ben said.

"Little known fact about me, Ben, but I have three sisters. Roller skating was big when I was growing up."

He shook his head a little. "Wow, three sisters, that's gotta be …"

"Nuts," Esther piped up, and Ben and I both broke out in giggles.

I tapped her nose. "It was nuts sometimes, but in a good way. I love my sisters and they loved having a baby brother to boss around."

"Ben likes bossing me around," Esther said matter of fact, and I chuckled.

"That comes with being a big brother," I reminded her and she rested her hand on her chin.

"But I wanted to give mom a hug this morning

and he said I couldn't. He made me sit at the table and color."

I glanced at Ben. "Is that true?"

"Yes, but I wasn't trying to be mean. It seemed like the nicer we were, the sadder she got. I thought it would be smart to let her be for a little bit and see if she would stop crying."

"Hmm, I guess I can see your way of thinking. Can you see what he was thinking, Esther?" I asked the girl, and she shrugged.

"I guess so, but it was us who made her sad, so I thought we should fix her."

I leaned on the table and looked at both of them. "How did you make her sad?"

Ben shifted uncomfortably and gave the *don't say a word* look to Esther. I waited for one of them to talk, but Esther wouldn't look up from her pop glass and Ben was drumming out a beat on the table with his fingers.

"You know I can't help her if I don't know what the problem is, right?"

Ben finally looked me in the eye. "I think it has something to do with Jacob."

I raised one brow. "You mean your dad."

"No, I mean Jacob. Mom said I don't have to call him Dad anymore. She said if I feel that strongly about it, then I can call him Jacob. He's never been a dad to me or Esther."

"When did you talk about this?"

"Last night," Esther answered. "Mom said the lawyer called and then she and Ben got in an argument about name-calling."

I saw the look of fear in Ben's eyes, as though I was going to scold him for making things difficult for his mom.

"I guess you have every right to feel the way you do, Ben. As long as you're respectful and your mom agrees."

"She does," he promised, looking relieved.

The waitress interrupted our conversation to take our order and when she left, Ben snapped his fingers. "Sasha!"

"Excuse me?" I asked surprised and he frowned.

"Your middle name isn't Sasha?" I shook my head. "Simba? Sassafras?"

"None of the above, my boy," I laughed. "Nice try, though."

"I will come up with it," he swore.

"Will you two excuse me for just a second? I want to make a phone call and when I get back, we're going to eat some pizza!"

They waved and I walked to the corner of the room where it was quiet. Then, I dialed the number of the only other person who could help me figure this out.

"Where are you, beautiful?" I called from the

front door when I closed it behind me.

"I'm in the kitchen," she called and I strolled through, my hands in my pockets. I came up behind her at the sink and put my arms around her waist, kissing her neck.

"Mmm, you smell good," I whispered, my breath blowing on her neck.

"That's not me, it's the cookies I baked. Where are the kids? They usually aren't so quiet."

She turned to look up at me and I kissed her lips. "They aren't here. They're having a sleepover with your parents. They're going to take them to church and you can pick them up when you go to Sunday dinner. Well, when we go to Sunday dinner."

"You called my parents and asked them to take my kids?" she reiterated.

"I did, both tired little roller rink rats. They were happy to spend time with Jo-Jo and Sunny. Adam was going to teach them how to make a new cupcake he created."

She laughed. "My poor mother. She's going to have a mess on her hands."

"She didn't seem overly worried about it," I promised.

"Wait, they don't have any clothes with them," she said, her hands going to her back pockets.

"I took them to the store and got them an outfit for tomorrow. Your mom said you should really start keeping clothes there for them."

She stepped back and leaned against the counter. "She did?"

I nodded. "It makes sense. Now that they won't be going to Jacob's, they will have more weekends to spend at the Alexander farm."

She threw the towel down on the counter and stomped toward the living room. "I didn't ask you to take over control of my children, Nick!"

She was through the door before I had a chance to react. What was going on with her? My anger flared and I strode through the house, catching her arm as she was going into her bedroom. "What in the hell is your problem?" I asked, spinning her around to face me. "God help anyone who tries to help you, Mandy Alexander!"

I let go of her arm, walked to the front door, and slammed it behind me.

Chapter Nineteen

My house was dark and chilled when I opened the front door, so I turned up the fireplace in the living room and went to the kitchen for a drink. What the hell is going on with her? One minute she's her usual sweet self, and the next minute she's Queen B of the Universe again. Trying to figure it out was giving me a headache. Maybe she just needed time alone without the kids or me encroaching on her space, so she could figure it out.

I took a drink of the amber liquid that scorched my throat going down. I dumped the rest down the drain and braced my arms on the counter. Using alcohol to relax was a mistake I wasn't willing to make. Social drinking was okay, but drinking when you're angry is never a good idea.

I sank down on the couch and stared into the fire. I saw her face this morning when I went over and she looked gutted from life. I saw her face just now when I yelled at her. It was a cross between sadness and fear. She was scared. Not of me, but definitely of something.

I stood and flipped the fireplace off, going to the front door. I had to work this out with her while the kids weren't there to distract us. I pulled the door open and she was standing on the stoop, her hand raised to knock. She dropped it quickly when she saw me standing there. The look on her face was enough to break my heart and I pulled her to me, hugging her tenderly.

"I'm sorry I lost my temper," I whispered, wishing she would wrap her arms around me instead of standing like a statue.

"I'm not having a good day," she whispered back.

"Do you want to come in and talk about it?" I asked, unsure what my next move should be.

"No, because I don't want you to stop loving me and … and …"

I kissed her temple and rubbed her back for a moment. "I'm not going to stop loving you because you've had a bad day."

"You should. You should just leave and find someone with less baggage, Nick."

I held in the sigh I felt deep in my chest and pulled her through the door, closing it behind us. I put my arm around her shoulder and walked with her to the living room where I flipped the fireplace back on, and sat her on the couch. "Would you like a glass of wine?"

She shook her head. "Thank you, but no. It would probably make me sick the way I'm feeling right now."

I sat next to her and leaned forward on my thighs, concentrating on the flames of the fire.

"How are you feeling right now?"

"Like karma has come home to roost and I'm a terrible person. That all the choices I've made have doomed me to a life of pain and suffering. I can't make anyone happy and never will make anyone happy, including my children. There is so much pain in my chest that I can hardly breathe most of the time. I thought I couldn't hurt worse than I did when I found Jacob cheating on me, but I was wrong."

"I'm at a disadvantage here. I don't know what happened to make you think karma is out for you, but I know you aren't a terrible person. You make me very happy, and your kids think you hang the sun and the moon. I won't even get into the number of kids you have helped over the years in the district. Will you tell me what's gone on since you left school yesterday? The kids said you got a call from your lawyer, and after that, you and Ben got in an argument."

"It wasn't an argument as much as it was Ben drawing a line in the sand when it comes to his father."

"But if Jacob is going to be out of your life, does it really matter?" I asked, perplexed.

She wouldn't look at me, but her chin gave her away when it vibrated enough to tell me she was holding back tears.

"He's not going to be out of your life, right?" I asked quietly and she shook her head, sucking in a breath as though she had been holding it for days.

"Kate said the state won't allow him to sign away his parental rights. They believe the only reason he's doing it is to get out of his obligation to pay child support. The state would only allow him to waive his parental rights if there was someone else waiting in the wings to adopt them. Otherwise, they say the kids could become burdens of the state if I had to go on public assistance."

I put my arm around her shoulder and held her until she laid her head on my chest. "But you won't need to do that. You have a good job and do just fine without Jacob."

She nodded and tucked her hand under her cheek against my chest. "Right now, I do, but if I ever got laid off, or my legs caused a major problem and I couldn't work …"

I rested my head on top of hers. "Now, you feel completely hopeless because no one believes you can do this alone."

She nodded and took another deep breath, only this time she didn't speak.

"I believe you can do this alone, Mandy. I know you don't need that piece of trash to support your kids, nor do you want him to. It might take the state a little while to see that, but eventually, they will. He's in California now, so you don't have to send the kids to him at least, right?"

"Kate filed a change in the custody papers. She claimed sending the kids to Jacob now was unrealistic as the agreement stands since he's on the other side of the country. She also petitioned the court to remove his right for unsupervised visits after what happened to Esther. The judge agreed that the children were not safe with him, so they can only see him at a safe place facility within twenty-five miles of their custodial parent's home."

"But he doesn't live in the state anymore. How does that work?"

She shook her head. "It doesn't, which is what we wanted. He will have to come back here anytime he wants to see the kids. He doesn't want to see the kids, so he will never come back. That's the only good part about this. My kids won't have to see him again unless he moves back here for some reason. In the meantime, they are free from having to deal with him."

"That's some good news. We don't have to worry about them getting hurt."

"We?" she asked, and I nodded.

"Yeah, we, Mandy. I love your kids and I love you. I wish you had come and talked to me about this last night. I would have told you that I personally think Jacob's life is where karma is roosting. I spent the whole day with Ben and Esther today, and we had so much fun. Esther and I skated for hours at the rink while Ben hung out with his friends. He and I did things boys and their dads do together, like trying to beat each other at foosball and tag-teaming each other during the skate-off race. Your kids are wonderful, Mandy, and that's because of you, not Jacob. I'm honored to spend time with them. His loss is my gain, as far as I'm concerned."

"You skated with Esther?" she asked as though that was all she got from everything that I said.

"She wanted to go roller skating, but with her arm still healing, I didn't dare let her on the floor alone, so I carried her. We skated when she wasn't in the middle of the rink using the turtle racers."

"I wish I had been there to see that."

"Ben took pictures." I winked and she smiled then.

"That's what dads are supposed to do. Dads aren't supposed to scar their children for life." She was smiling finally and I took her hand.

"No, they aren't. I think you've had a bit of a hard time with dads between your own and Jacob. I think the difference is, your dad did what he did because he couldn't deal with the aftermath of the accident. He couldn't deal with the way it made him feel to see his little girl lying in a hospital bed, missing her feet. That doesn't make it right, but it makes it easier to understand. Jacob did what he did because he was a coward, nothing more. It had nothing to do with you or your children, and everything to do with him. That much is obvious, considering how willing he was to sign away his rights."

"I should have seen right through that. I should have seen that he was just trying to relieve himself of the burden he's been carrying around all these years."

I rubbed her back and kissed her forehead. "Sometimes, we get caught up in the idea that we can finally be free of something that has been dragging us down, and we focus on one spot instead of the big picture. I will testify if you need me to that the kids aren't safe with him. I have no problem doing that. I was there and heard everything that Ben said. I'm a mandatory reporter for abuse, so I will gladly let the court know what I saw."

She rubbed my chest in a slow pattern before she spoke. "Thank you, but I don't think it will be necessary. The judge already changed the visitation rights to supervised only, so that means he knows the kids aren't safe with him. I can't ask for more than that. If Jacob shows up over the holidays, or in the summer, and wants to see them, I have to let them, but at least they won't be alone with him."

"Okay, that's good enough for now. Someday, he will be gone from your life, I promise you."

I kissed her lips, letting mine warm her cold ones and she broke away, resting her head on my chest.

"No, he won't, that's what you don't understand. The judge from the civil case found out he wasn't paying for my legs. They arrested him, Nick."

I hugged her closer to me. "I'm sorry."

She struggled out of my arms and stood, pacing to the fireplace and looking at the pictures of my sisters on the mantle. "I'm not upset that they arrested him."

I chuckled. "I didn't think you were. I said I'm sorry because I know it feels like everything is dumping on you right now when it comes to him."

"It is. First, he was arrested for being in contempt of court, then they released him after he begged his mommy and daddy for the money. For two sets of legs, that's to the tune of nearly ten grand."

"But if he had the money, he would have been paying for them all along."

"Exactly!" She threw her hands up in the air and when they came down, she wrapped them in her hair. "The court doesn't really care, though. They said if he doesn't pay me back, he will go to jail as it is spelled out in the court papers. That's just asinine. If he's in jail, there's no way he can pay his child support, or for the legs. Why is the law so dumb?"

I gave her the palms up. "I don't know, but I agree that it's asinine. What happens next?"

"Well, good news for you, because you're going to get your money back for the legs. I had to fax Kate the charges this morning and Jacob's parents paid the nearly ten thousand, which they can't afford either, by the way. So, he's out of jail, and now they're drafting a payroll deduct for my legs."

I stood and went to her, taking her hand, "I don't understand."

"They decided since he couldn't be trusted to

pay when I needed them, then they would pull the money from his check every month to go into a fund. They did a complicated mathematical equation that told them how much to deduct monthly that would continue to pay for the legs for the rest of my life. So, on top of the child support, he has to pay that out of his check. He's an angry, unhappy man, according to his mother."

"While I can understand that he's unhappy, I'm not sad that he will be forced to pay. That takes one more burden off your back. If the money goes into an account, then you don't have to deal with him, right?"

She shook her head. "At least not when it comes to my legs."

I kissed her forehead, afraid that she would reject anything more. "I don't want the money back, Mandy. Donate it to the coat drive or keep it in case you or the kids need something."

She gazed up at me and looked long and hard into my eyes. "Would it be okay if I give it back to his parents then? They had to draw off their investments to get it and they can't afford to lose that kind of money. They just can't. Besides, they shouldn't have to suffer because of something their son did."

I sighed and shook my head. "I'm not a parent, but I think sometimes, when your child does something so morally wrong that they hurt someone as badly as he hurt you, then there was something missing in their parenting. In this case, the accident was just that, an accident, and I can't hold them responsible for his poor decisions when it came to ending your marriage. I respect that they did the right thing and gave you the money, but I suspect it was because they didn't want their son to sit in jail. That said, you may give them back the money I paid for this new set of legs, but I must insist you keep the money from the last set you paid for. I know you can use it with Christmas coming, right?"

She nodded. "But, I feel guilty about keeping it, Nick."

I caressed her cheek and smiled. "I know because you're an honest person, Mandy. Do you have bills to pay from Esther's accident?"

Her lips curled into a small grin. "Funny thing about that. I went to set up a payment plan and the billing department told me there was no balance."

"Well, that's sorted. Consider it one less thing to worry about."

"Nick, did you pay Esther's hospital bill? I know it was getting close to two thousand dollars. I told you not to do that."

"I told you, and your father, I would do whatever I could to help ease the burden right now. I meant it. I think you should use some of the money from Jacob's parents and pay off any bills you might have left from her treatment, buy the kids new clothes or whatever they may need, and save the rest for a rainy day. Their grandparents aren't going to object to the money being used to help their grandchildren, especially when Esther was hurt on their watch."

"Okay, you're right. I was thinking maybe if they have to be financially responsible for his mistakes, they might stop enabling him so much. Does that make me a bad person?"

I took her face in my hands and kissed her, not caring if she rejected me or not. She didn't, she leaned into it and returned the kiss with the same kind of hunger I felt.

I ended the kiss and lowered my brow. "It doesn't make you a bad person at all. It makes you the kind of parent they should have been. Don't feel bad about the mistakes they made. You can't change them. I'm sure they will appreciate getting part of the money back and they will think twice about helping him in the future."

She nodded firmly. "We can hope. I'm sorry for being such a downer. I don't feel like I can talk to my family about this since they already don't like Jacob, so I hold it inside and then turn into a weepy mess."

"You aren't a downer and you can always talk to me about it. Don't feel like just because he's your ex that I don't care about what's going on. I do care, a lot. I love you. I don't want you to carry a burden alone when you don't have to. We will get through this and we'll deal with Jacob together when things come up. That's what two people who are in love do. I want what's best for Esther and Ben."

She threw up a hand. "What's best for them is to have Jacob out of their lives for good!"

I caught the hand as it was going to her side and held it to my chest. "Since that's not possible right now, we will do everything we can to make sure they are happy and have good male role models in their lives. We'll take everything else one day at a time, okay?"

"I'll try to do that, the taking one day at a time part. That's hard for me sometimes."

I pulled her into me and kissed the top of her head. "I know. You've been a mom and a dad to those two kids for so long. You always have to plan ahead and be ready for anything. I hope you'll let me take a little part of that burden now and trust me with your heart and theirs."

She ran her hand down my face and stared into my eyes for several long minutes. "I do trust you with my heart and theirs, or you wouldn't have taken them away from me today, and I wouldn't be here telling you this now. I know you aren't going to break my heart the way he did because you …" She paused as though she was looking for the right word.

"Because I cherish you, Mandy. That's the honest truth."

She slipped her arms around my waist and hugged me. "I love you so much, Nick. It scares me sometimes how much I've come to depend on you emotionally. I'm changing because of your love. I laugh more. Enjoy music more. I eat better and take better care of my legs. Most of all, though, is the change I've noticed in Ben since you started spending so much time with him. He's more confident and doesn't think the world is out to get him. He's so optimistic about a future with you that it scares me sometimes. It will break his heart if this doesn't end well between us."

I held her out by the shoulders and stared at her under one brow. "Neither your son nor you are going to get your heart broken by me. It's probably funny that my biggest fear is the same as Ben's."

"That his heart will get broken if things don't work out between us?" she asked, confused.

"No, that my heart will get broken if you decide to stop loving me."

She shook her head gently at first, then more vigorously. "I miss you so much sometimes it hurts."

"I'm always right here. I know it's hard with the kids and wanting to make sure they are comfortable with our relationship, but maybe it's time to let them see us be more loving with each other. We both tend to stay pretty hands-off when I'm at your house in the evenings, so maybe more hand-holding and hugs would make all of us more secure in how we feel about each other."

She laughed for the first time all day. "I know it would for me."

"It won't be hard for me. What's hard is not hugging you. Well, that's not the only thing that's hard most of the time." I winked and she snickered.

"I noticed. We're alone for the whole night. How about if you make love to me for the majority of it?"

"Oh, don't worry, I intend to make love to you for a very long time tonight, but that's later."

"Later? Can't we just close the door to your bedroom and pretend there is nothing on the outside to worry about?"

I took her hand and led her to my bedroom. She sat on the bed while I pulled a duffle bag from the closet and threw in some essentials then grabbed my suit zipped up in a suit protector. She was staring at me rather funny and when I finished, I picked up the duffel bag and the suit, took her other hand and led her out the front door, locking it behind me. We strolled past the driveway to her front door and repeated the process. This time, I sat on her bed and motioned for her to pack.

"Pack a bag, please. We don't have to be at your parents' until twelve-thirty tomorrow. It's only four. We're running away."

She glanced nervously toward the kids' rooms. "I don't want to be too far away …"

"We won't be. We're going to Rochester; that's not far from here."

"You don't want to stay at home with me?"

I stood and rubbed her arms up and down. "I don't mind staying home with you, but when we have a chance to go out without the kids, I want to show off the beautiful woman on my arm. I want other men to be jealous that I have the most amazing woman. I want to feed you gourmet food and make you heady on fine wine. Then I want to take you back to our hotel room and kiss every inch of your skin. I want to massage your sweet breasts in my hands while I taste you on my tongue until I can't stand the torture any longer and plunge myself deep inside you."

She shivered under my hands and got a look in her eye that told me I was going to get exactly what I wanted.

Chapter Twenty

"I'm so full," she whisper-moaned against my shoulder as I held her on the dance floor. "I haven't eaten that much food in years."

I rested my hands on her bottom. "Maybe you've just gotten used to those horrible pretzels and forgot what a good meal can do for the soul."

She laughed freely. "Maybe, or maybe you kept refilling my wine glass to get me drunk so you could have your way with me."

"I don't need to get you drunk to have my way with you. I was simply enjoying our time alone together."

She laid her head back on my shoulder while we slow danced in the corner of the room to a Frank Sinatra tune. "I know it's hard dating a single mom who can't send her kids off every other weekend to their father's."

I crossed my arms across her back and held her waist. "Don't misconstrue why we are here, Mands. I would have been happy in Snowberry fixing the three of you dinner and watching Frozen for the four hundredth time if your mom and dad hadn't taken the kids. The reason we're here is to make you feel like you aren't a single mom, even if it's only for a night. I want you to feel like you have no responsibilities and not a care in the world other than being with the man you love. With the man who makes you cry out his name when he brings you to completion every time he lies with you."

"Sex in the city," she said, gazing up into my face.

"I never watched that show, but I can assure you there will be sex in the city tonight. Only it will be more like long, slow, sensuous sex."

"I think we should go now, please," she begged, pressing her belly into my now uncomfortable suit pants.

I turned my back to the floor and pressed her up against the wall, pretending we were still dancing. "We'll have to wait a few minutes until my pants don't look like an adolescent teen's at prom. But, as soon as I can, I'm going to walk you out of this place and down the street to our room. I'm going to draw you a bubble bath and then wash you, running my hands over your shoulders and down to your soft breasts."

She gave half a smile. "I can't take a bath. I can't get in and out of the tub."

I laughed wickedly. "That's really not a problem. I can put you in the tub, and then you're captive there until I take you out, to make love to you. That is if I take you out before I make love to you."

I lowered my lips to hers and she reacted, kissing me hungrily and whining in the back of her throat to drive me almost to the brink of embarrassing myself on a dance floor. I tore my lips from hers and leaned my forehead on the wall, her body trapped under me and our breath labored.

"That sound you make is like lighter fluid to fire, Mands. All I can think about is the feel of you around me."

I took her hand and pulled her from the dance floor then stopped for our coats and her purse at the coatroom. I pushed the door open for her and we stepped out into the cool November air. I took her hand and forced my steps to match hers, which wasn't easy when I wanted to swing her up over my shoulder like a caveman and carry her back to the room.

"Well, if it isn't the principal and his pet."

My steps faltered and I turned on one heel to face Cindy Arsenault. Mandy withered next to me and I kept my arm around her waist. If this woman ruins my night, I might just choke her.

"Are you following us, Cindy?" I asked, surprised to see her.

"Don't flatter yourself, Nick. There are such things as coincidences in life."

"If that's the case, then enjoy your night."

I turned, still holding Mandy's waist, and Cindy caught her arm on her way around. "Just a tip for you, Mandy, sleeping with the boss doesn't get you anywhere in the education community. It tends to make enemies, instead."

Mandy shrunk back instinctively and I ground

my teeth together. "Once again, Cindy, I am not Mandy's boss. You seem to be the only one who has a problem understanding that. If you have an issue with our behavior, you know who you can speak to about it. However, it would be wise to remember the old saying *those who live in glass houses shouldn't throw stones.*"

I scooped Mandy past her and turned our backs, walking away as quickly as her legs would allow us to. "Don't look back and just keep walking," I said out the side of my lip.

I was pleased that she held her head high, even though I know she was angry and hurt. I pulled the door open to the hotel and held it for her. I turned my head and Cindy stood in the same place, her body held in a way that told me she was thinking very hard about her next play on the board. I made sure we made eye contact, and then I followed Mandy in the door and shut Cindy out of my mind.

Mandy sat on the edge of the bed, sipping a glass of wine while I filled the corner hot tub. "She's going to report back to Neal and Warren. You know that, right?"

I stood and loosened my tie while the tub filled. "Let her, they're both aware of our relationship and neither of them has a problem with it."

"They are?" she asked in complete surprise, almost spilling her wine. I caught it just before it tipped to the floor.

I turned the water off and threw my tie on the bed. "Do you remember the last time we stayed in a hotel together, and I told you I would leave Snowberry if that's what had to happen in order for us to be together?" She nodded, but her wine glass shook, giving her away. I took it from her hand and set it on the table next to the bed. "I went to Neal and Warren the next week and asked them if they had a problem with me dating you."

"I'm still surprised that they didn't, to be honest."

I caressed her face and reached around behind her to unbutton the top of her dress, "Yet, when I asked, both of them chuckled and said it was about time." I lowered the zipper on the dress and she shivered as the teeth chattered down. "I kind of think they had a bet going. I suspected when I left Warren's office, one of the two of them had to pay up."

"You're staying in Snowberry, is that what you're saying?" she asked, her voice breathy.

"That's exactly what I'm saying. Now, how about I take this new dress off and make you pay up?"

She stood and the dress pooled around her ankles. I stooped and rather than pull her legs out of her dress, I unstrapped the plates at her ankles and lifted her from the sockets. She clung to my neck and I laid my lips on hers. I walked backward until I could set her on the edge of the tub.

"You're going to *make* me pay up?" she asked as my hands worked her out of the skimpy bra she was wearing.

"I am, and it's going to cost you," I warned, kissing her neck as the bra fell away. I tossed it behind me and stood back, eyeing the woman before me. I unbuttoned my shirt very slowly while she sat there naked but for her thong. Her eyes trailed my fingers as they went through the buttons until the last one gave and the shirt fell open. "Ready to get in the water yet?" I asked, crooking a brow.

She twisted to the side and dipped her hands in the bubbles, running her wet hands down her chest. "I've been ready, but you won't quit talking."

She swung her legs into the water and sank to the bottom. In seconds, her thong joined the dress and I groaned, shaking my head.

"You are a little minx, woman," I moaned, stripping my shirt off and tossing it to the ground behind me.

She rested her head on the edge of the tub and I leaned over, kissing her neck. She jolted upward and I grabbed her face, holding her steady. I slid my hands down her bubble slick body until my hands closed over her breasts. She moaned and I was in the water next to her before I had another conscious thought. When her hand went to my zipper, I didn't even care that my suit pants cost two hundred bucks a pair.

Chapter Twenty-One

I checked my phone and tried not to groan when I saw that it was barely noon. The day had spun out of control when a student was injured on the playground at morning recess and his mother was less than understanding. She seemed to think that my recess monitor should have known he was going to jump off the swing and break an arm. It was time to lock myself in my office and eat lunch before I lost my temper from hunger.

I strode toward the staff lunchroom to heat it and heard angry words being exchanged. I recognized both of them and immediately opened the camera app on my iPhone. It was time to end this once and for all. Thankful that the ringer was off, and they couldn't hear the video start, I stood to the side of the door and listened.

"I'm really tired of your pity party, Mandy," Cindy said in a seething voice.

"I'm not having a pity party, Cindy. I never have. I think you have me confused with someone else."

Cindy cackled in a way that sent a shiver up my spine. "I know exactly who I'm talking to. You may have Nick fooled, but I know the truth. You're nothing more than a drunken whore who thinks she can use her missing feet as a way to hold a man's heart in her hand."

I forced my feet to move back the way I came, so I didn't get caught eavesdropping by Cindy. I stopped at the office and stuck my head in the door. "I gotta run next door, Louis. I'll be back in a few minutes."

"You got it, boss," he answered, giving me a distracted salute.

I didn't have my coat and the bite of the November wind cut through my dress shirt as I jogged to central office. I pushed through the door and stopped at the receptionist's desk.

"Hey, Nick. Where's the fire?" Tiffany asked jokingly until I turned my gaze to her. "You need to see Warren?"

"Now," I answered, irritated that she even had to ask.

She picked up her phone and spoke for a moment, then hung up and motioned me back to his office.

I strode through the door and closed it behind me. "Sorry to interrupt, Warren."

"No, you're not. If you were sorry, you wouldn't be acting like a Neanderthal."

I chose to ignore him and tossed my phone on his desk, the video open. "We have a problem."

He picked up the phone and watched the video, his lips in a thin line. When it finished, he glanced up at me. "Where did you get this and when?"

I sat in the chair across from him, barely balancing on the edge. "I was walking back to my office just now and when I approached the staff break room, I heard them. I stood to the side and recorded it. They had no idea I was there."

Warren sat back and steepled his fingers, "So they don't know you were recording them?"

"No, but what difference does that make? Mandy told me this has been going on for years."

He leaned forward immediately. "What? Cindy has been harassing her for years?"

"According to Mandy, yes. She said Cindy has called her an entitled cripple since her accident. Apparently, she only says it when they are alone together. It's escalated a lot recently."

"What does that mean?" Warren asked, tapping a pen on his blotter pad.

"Mandy and I ran into Cindy in St. Paul at MEA. She made some insulting and inappropriate comments. I squashed her and told her it was none of her business what Mandy and I were doing together. Last weekend, Mandy and I were in Rochester and Cindy ran into us."

"Like with her car?" he asked perplexed.

I laughed for the first time since I got there. "No, we were walking down the sidewalk and she was there suddenly."

"I see, and what happened?"

"She called Mandy the principal's pet and then told her that sleeping with the boss won't make her any friends in the education community. I told her to feel free to talk to you about it because you knew we were dating, and she became furious."

Warren leaned back again and banged his head on the chair a few times. "Do you think it was a coincidence that she was there?"

"Honestly, I want to say yes, but both times the only way she could have known we were there was if she was following us or somehow keeping an eye on what we were doing. MEA wouldn't be too hard, everyone was in St. Paul that night, but I booked a room in a hotel no one from Snowberry was staying in for that reason. Last weekend, I can't explain unless she overheard me telling Ben and Esther that I was going to take their mom to Rochester, which is possible. We were in public."

"This can't continue, Nick. We're letting her get away with something we suspend and expel students for. I won't stand for bullying by students or teachers."

I nodded. "I agree. I warned her she had one strike left, but I don't think she believed me. She seems to think she's untouchable."

"Call her over here," he said, motioning to his phone.

I picked up the receiver and punched in Louis's extension, waiting while it rang. When he finally picked up, he was out of breath. "Louis, it's Nick."

"Hi, sir, we have a problem over here."

I stood and looked through the window in the office. "What kind of problem?"

"I don't really know what happened, but I went to the breakroom to have lunch and Mandy was lying on the floor hurt, and Cindy was standing over her."

My heart stopped beating. "Did you call an ambulance?"

"She wouldn't let me. She said she was okay, but she's not. I think she might have hurt her arm. I had to help her to your office. I was just about to call you."

"Where's Cindy now?" I asked, hating that I was tied to the phone with the cord.

"I sent her back to class. She claimed Mandy fell and she was helping her, but Mandy isn't talking, sir."

"Warren and I will be right over. Keep Mandy in my office and get someone to cover her class."

"Yes, sir," he said, hanging up.

I grabbed my phone off Warren's desk and we both took off across the street while I explained what Louis told me.

Warren grabbed my arm and stopped me at the doors. "Fair warning, Nick, if Cindy assaulted Mandy, I will call the police."

I nodded once, my lips in a grim line because that was my suspicion, too. Louis wasn't at his desk when we walked in and we found him in our office, sitting with Mandy. She had an icepack on her arm and was slumped over in the chair.

"Sir, she says she's okay, but I think she should see a doctor," Louis said nervously.

"She will, as soon as we get to the bottom of this," I assured him.

"I'll be at my desk if you need anything, sir," he said, walking to the door.

"Louis," I called, and he stopped at the door, "why are you calling me sir?"

"I, uh, I… I'm nervous, sir," Louis answered.

I sat next to Mandy in the chair he had vacated. "Well, stop, would you? It's creeping me out."

Louis's laugh was forced, but he nodded. "Right, sorry, boss."

He closed the door and I took the icepack off Mandy's wrist. The wrist was swollen and mottled.

"What happened, love?" I asked, rubbing one hand down her face. She was almost in a trance as Warren sat in my desk chair.

"I was just having lunch," she said, breathing shallow and speaking so softly I could barely hear her. "I don't normally eat here, but I had extra time, so I wanted to work on the music program. I was almost done eating when Cindy came in."

I opened my phone and showed her the video. When it finished, she was in tears. "I was over showing this to Warren, which is why I wasn't here."

She glanced at Warren, fear radiating off of her. "I didn't start anything, I swear. I got up to leave when she came in and started her usual garbage with me."

Warren leaned forward and smiled. "Mandy, I believe you. Just tell us what happened so we can get you some medical attention."

"Right after that video," she pointed at the phone, "I stood to leave. I usually never say anything to her, but I had enough today. After last weekend, when you know she didn't just bump into us, I decided it had to end."

"What did you do?" I asked slowly.

"I stood up for myself for once. That's what I did. I told her I wasn't going to put up with her bullying any longer, and I wasn't going to let her put me down anymore."

"Did you push her?" I asked.

Her eyes got huge and she tried to stand, but I grabbed hold of her shoulder.

"No! No, I didn't touch her," she cried, the shock seeming to wear off. "I really don't remember what happened because the next thing I knew, I was on the floor. It happened so fast. She must have pushed me, and you know I don't have good balance if I'm caught off guard. She said she had enough of me trying to take her man and then kicked me hard in the side. That's why I'm sitting this way, my side hurts."

Warren and I both stood and she pulled up her shirt a bit. There was a softball size bruise covering her lower abdomen and disappearing down to her hip.

"I don't know what would have happened if Louis hadn't walked in," Mandy said, letting the shirt fall again. "She's going to deny it all, of course."

Warren picked up the phone and punched a few numbers. "This is Warren Leafson from Snowberry School District. I need an ambulance and police officer at John Peter Thomas Elementary School. Please, no sirens, and have them park at the back of the school. Someone will escort them from there." He gave them the pertinent information and hung up.

"Warren, I don't think that's necessary," Mandy tried to object and he stood again, kneeling by her chair.

"I do, Mandy. You're obviously injured and need to see a doctor. How are your legs? You said you were unbalanced."

"They feel bruised, but that happens when I fall. They'll be fine, but I can't bend down to check them."

"What's not fine is that this has gone on for so long. I'm giving you fair warning. I'm having Cindy arrested for assault."

Mandy jumped toward him but quickly fell to the side in pain. "Don't do that Warren," she huffed, her breath coming in short spurts. "I'll never be able to work with her again."

Warren laughed and shook his head as though Mandy was the funniest comic on the tour. "Mandy, she's not going to be working here. Once she's arrested, that's an automatic suspension while the charges are investigated."

"No one saw it, Warren. Let it go," she winced and I tried to hold her head, so she was more comfortable. I kissed her forehead and fought against closing my eyes from the pain of knowing I could have stopped this. Warren opened the door and spoke with Louis while I comforted Mandy.

"We have cameras everywhere, Mands, including in the breakroom. The investigation is going to be short and justice will be quick. Your job is to get better, so you can be ready for the Christmas program," I whispered, trying to calm her, but at the mention of her job, she struggled to stand, only to moan a little when she moved her side.

"I'm late for class. I have to go." She tried to fight against me and I held her tightly.

"Your class is taken care of. You need to see a doctor and take a day to feel better. The kids will be fine."

"What about Ben and Esther?" she asked. "I can't go to the hospital. I have to pick them up after school."

Warren came back into the room. "Mandy, we'll make sure Ben and Esther are picked up. Louis called your dad and he's waiting at the hospital to check you out. Let the paramedics do their job and we will do ours. I'll send Nick to get the kids once we have this taken care of and he will bring them to you."

Mandy moaned when she tried to sit up straighter. She peeked up at me from under her bangs. "I don't have a choice, do I?"

I laughed and kissed her cheek. "Afraid not, love. I want to come with you, but I have to take care of this. You understand, right?"

She nodded. "Of course, and I'm fine, really. You're both overreacting."

"I think we should be the judge of that," a man said from the doorway and Mandy groaned.

"Bram? How did you find out about this? You don't ride the rigs."

"When an Alexander name comes over a 911 call, we hear about it. Dad called and insisted I come and escort you to the hospital. He's waiting there for us."

Mandy rolled her eyes. "Great, Dully will be next."

Bram stood to the side so the paramedic could come through. "He called, but I insisted he stay at the middle school. He couldn't find anyone to take his class."

I stepped aside while the paramedic did a quick assessment. He took the icepack off her arm and applied a splint to it then addressed her side before he spoke to her. "Does it hurt to move your side?" Mandy nodded, her face pinched with pain. "If we take you out the back, are you willing to ride on the stretcher?"

Mandy struggled to sit up. "No, really, I can walk."

Bram snorted when she fell back into the chair and I gave him a scathing look. "I'll carry her." I scooped her up carefully and she laid her head on my chest and panted with each breath. I tried to be careful of her side, but I knew I was causing her pain.

"Warren, I want Cindy in this office when I get back."

Chapter Twenty-Two

Bram held the door while I carried Mandy through to the waiting ambulance.

The paramedic pulled the doors open and pulled the stretcher down. "We will have to strap her on out here and then take her into the rig on the stretcher."

I laid her down gently and she curled onto her right side, squeezing her eyes shut.

"Mandy, you'll have to lie on your back," Bram said gently and Mandy shook her head.

"I can't, Bram. Hurts," she puffed quietly, and the paramedic started strapping her down the way she was laying.

"We gotta get her in the rig and the oxygen on. She needs a CT scan to check for internal bleeding," he said, shoving us aside.

He finished his work and he and Bram bumped the stretcher into the back carefully. Mandy moaned and I jumped in behind them, holding her hand while the paramedic put an oxygen mask over her nose. "You're going to be okay. I'll be there in just a few minutes. It won't take long here. Your Dad and December will take good care of you, so let them."

"We gotta roll, Nick," Bram said patiently and I nodded, kissing her forehead one last time before getting out of the rig. The doors shut and they pulled out of the parking lot. When the sirens started at the end of the block, my gut clenched. I forced myself not to think about it when a cop car pulled into the parking lot.

"What's going on, Nick?" he called as he grabbed his computer.

I jogged over to Officer Cloud and pointed toward the ambulance. "We have a situation, but you missed the victim. She's on her way to the hospital."

He pulled out his notebook. "What happened?"

I motioned him in the door. "Come with me and I'll tell you on the way."

"Mom, I don't want to go with Grandma. I want to stay here with you," Esther cried, hugging her mom carefully.

I knelt down next to where she sat on the bed and rubbed her back. "We know you do, Esther, but remember how at the hospital Grandpa told us mom needs to rest?" Esther nodded, but a big crocodile tear streaked down her face. "And remember when he said if she gets to rest, she will feel better tomorrow?"

"Yes, but I'll be real good and not ask for anything."

I smiled and held her hand. "You're always really good, sweetheart. It's just going to be boring here. Grandma Suzie could use your help at the house with the Thanksgiving dinner preparations. It's less than a week away. We need you to help, or we won't have turkey in our belly on Thursday."

Mandy took Esther's other hand and patted it. "Nick is going to stay with me, honey. I'll be just fine. You should go with Grandma and have a little fun, the way we planned. I'll be feeling better tomorrow and then you and Ben can come home."

Esther jumped down off the bed and hugged Mandy around the neck. "Okay, mom. Can I call you before I go to bed?"

Mandy brushed a piece of hair out of her daughter's face. "Of course, just like you always do when you're not here. I'll be waiting for your call."

I handed Esther off to Suzie, who had helped me get Mandy situated after we got home. "Ben packed a bag for each of them. I'll send updates, so Miss Esther can enjoy her cooking time with you."

Suzie patted my shoulder. "Thanks, Nick. She'll be fine."

She blew Mandy a kiss and held the little girl's hand as they walked down the hallway. When I heard the front door close, I kicked off my shoes and joined her on the bed.

"Still doing okay? I know the ride back from

the hospital was probably painful."

She rolled her head towards me. "I'm good. I'm counting my blessings right now that things weren't worse. The doctor said my wrist sprain won't stop me from playing for the concert."

I held up a finger. "*If* you take care of it and don't overdo it."

She held up her good hand in surrender. "I'll use a recording for the practices over the next few weeks until my hand is feeling good again. I promise, Principal Klaus."

I kissed her gently, so thankful she was home with me after such a long day. I checked the icepack around her waist and it was still cold, so I didn't mess with it. "This, on the other hand, might be a bigger problem."

"You heard the doctor say it was just a contusion, and in a few days, I'll be feeling better."

I laughed and kissed her cheek before I settled in next to her. "What I heard him say was you have a huge contusion with extensive swelling and that your rib may be broken."

"But the CT scan suggested it wasn't, so to ice and take the ibuprofen as prescribed."

I grimaced. "I sound a little overprotective, don't I?" She nodded and I kissed her cheek again. "I love you and I was scared to death this afternoon when Louis said you were hurt. I shouldn't have left you there alone with her. I thought it would be like every other time and she would leave. I wanted to take the video to Warren and I didn't want Cindy to know I had witnessed it."

She used her good hand to hold mine to her chest. "You didn't know it would escalate this time, Nick. Heck, I didn't know that the game had changed when I decided to stand up for myself. I guess I should have seen it, but she's bugged me for so many years I got complacent."

"What are you talking about?" I asked, confused, and she lowered her lashes until her eyes were closed. "Mandy, what else did she say to you?"

"She told me I stole you out from under her and she was going to take you back," she whispered, almost gagging on the words. "I figured she would have spilled her guts to you and Warren as a way to get herself out of the jam she created."

I whistled and shook my head. "No, love, there's no getting out of this. Warren and I never had a chance to talk to her. She was arrested by Officer Cloud once he viewed the tape."

She turned her head to look at me. "What? I know Warren said he was going to have her arrested, but I thought he was kidding."

I caressed her face and kissed her lips softly. "Let's talk about this tomorrow when you've slept. I know the pain medication is probably making you groggy."

"Nick, now."

I debated whether or not I should tell her or wait until she felt better, but her determined eyes told me she wasn't going to rest until I did.

"After you left in the ambulance, Officer Cloud,

Warren, and I watched the tape. The school lawyer advised Warren not to call Cindy down to the office until he was there. After he viewed the tape, he had me call her down and Officer Cloud arrested her. This is out of the school's hands now, but you will have to give your statement."

She waved her good hand. "Wait, what did the tape show? I was there and I didn't think she would be arrested."

"Apparently, most people, Cindy included, didn't know that shoving and kicking a school official is fourth-degree assault and punishable by a year in jail."

"I had no idea," she whispered.

"Neither did I until Officer Cloud explained it. Unfortunately for Cindy, on the video just before this happened, she was using language to imply that the attack was based on your disability. That very well may add a year to her sentence. Either way, she's no longer the school district's problem. As soon as she was charged with assault, she forfeited her job because she was on probation from her last disciplinary incident."

She held her hand to her forehead. "I don't want her to be charged, Nick. This is going to make the district look really bad."

I took her hand down and held it. I knew she was upset, sore, and the medication was making her feel unstable.

"No, this is going to make Cindy look really bad. Neither Warren, myself or the lawyer, is the least bit concerned about the school's reputation. If anything, it's a cautionary tale to anyone who thinks violence is the answer to a problem. I'm just sorry I didn't insist we stop this before it got out of hand. I knew about it and I could have prevented this if I had talked to Cindy."

She laughed as though I was an incredibly stupid man. "Or sent her right over the edge. She could have come here and hurt me. She could have taken her anger out on Ben or Esther. I'll be the punching bag to keep my kids safe. If you want my opinion, and this isn't the drugs talking, I think if you had talked to her about being nice to me, this whole thing could have been a lot worse."

I leaned on my elbow and made eye contact with her. "I don't understand what you mean. I warned her several times she was looking at her third strike and her job would be gone."

"That's exactly what I mean. You told her that, but it was in a social situation, not in the school in your office. I think if you had pulled her in and accused her of bullying me, she may have done something far worse. She may have come to my house with a gun or a knife. She's not stable, Nick. I honestly feel like I got lucky today. If Louis hadn't walked in, I don't know what would have happened. It could have ended with me on the floor like it did, or it could have ended with me on a slab in the morgue. I couldn't get up from the floor when she knocked me down. I was at her mercy if no one heard me screaming."

I laid my arm across her chest and held her tightly. "You're right. I thank my lucky stars she was in a school where she couldn't have a weapon. Whatever the case, the doctor said you need to rest, so you're going to do that now while I hold you."

Her eyes were drifting closed, but she was fighting it. "What time is it? I don't want to miss Esther's call."

"She won't call for a few hours. Rest now and when you wake up, I'll make you some soup and you can check on the kids," I promised.

She was already sleeping before I finished my sentence and I rested my head against her back and let out a shuddered breath. This was far too close of a call for me to want to be anywhere but right here in this bed with her every night. How I was going to do that was what I had to figure out.

Chapter Twenty-Three

I handed the clean turkey platter to Tom to dry. "That's the last of the dishes." I pointed at the fancy dishwasher under the sink. "Why are we washing dishes when you have a perfectly good dishwasher?"

"Because my darling wife says you can't put her fine china in the dishwasher, that's why, but I think she just wants us to work off our dinner. My belly is so full I can hardly stand here."

"Tell me about it. Suzie is one hell of a cook. Apparently, it didn't wear off on Mandy." I chuckled and he laughed.

"Hey, she can cook gourmet food. Gourmet pretzels. As hard as Suzie tried, that girl wasn't interested in learning."

I leaned against the sink and dried my hands. "It's because she has a creative mind. She doesn't have time for mundane things when she could be creating beautiful music."

He tossed the towel onto the drainer and copied my posture. The living room was full of people in various stages of food coma while the kids ran around outside.

"Come to think of it, she was always playing one instrument or another while her mother was cooking dinner. Maybe you know her better than I think you do."

I smiled, *thank you for the opening, Mr. Alexander.*

"I know her very well, sir. As a matter of fact, I would like to ask you for permission to marry her."

Before the words were out of my mouth, he had my shirt in his hand and his face in mine. "Is this a shotgun wedding?"

I held my hands up and shook my head. "No, sir. I know we haven't been dating long, but we've known each other for five years. This isn't an imminent proposal, but when the time is right, I would like to know I have your permission."

"I see," he said, stepping back and smoothing the wrinkle from my shirt. "Well, in that case, I suppose we can talk about it. Let's go for a walk to my woodshop."

I grabbed my coat off the chair and on the way by the door, kissed Mandy on the cheek. "Be right back." I winked and she nodded. She looked better every day and I was happy to see she was relaxed and resting as she visited with the woman who had earned a night off dish duty.

Tom snapped his collar up around his neck and took off for the back of the property. I followed, waiting for him to talk, but wondered if that was simply a figure of speech. Maybe all we were doing here was witnessing his dominance, so I didn't get any ideas about hurting his daughter. He stopped at a building and opened a door, disappearing into the dark. A light came on and I stepped through the door as well, surprised by the extent of the woodshop that lay before me.

"I'm impressed," I admitted. "When you said woodshop, I was picturing a little corner of the garage."

He held his arms out. "When you have property this size, you might as well build what you want, no?"

"It's beautiful and I definitely envy you. I'm not much of a carpenter."

He motioned to a stool that sat under a long oak bar. He pulled a bottle off the shelf with two glasses and poured us each a glass of the amber liquid. I accepted the glass and he raised his, saying nothing, so I did the same. I drank the brandy slowly and enjoyed the smoothness as it went down.

"Don't like brandy, son?" he asked, already pouring himself a second.

"Just the opposite, sir, I love it. So much so I don't drink it very often. That way, I never fall out of love with it."

"Maybe it's time for you to call me Tom," he suggested, raising his glass again.

"Thank you, Tom. I appreciate being welcomed into the fold, even if it is tentatively."

He spun his glass on the high shine bar, "How long do you think it will be before you fall out of love with my daughter? Since you have her all the time, that is."

Dangerous waters ahead.

"If by *having her all the time* you mean spending every spare minute we can together as a family, then yes, that is the case. If by *having her all the time* you mean sharing her bed, then you're dead wrong."

He raised a brow. "Why is it she was injured on your watch if you love her so much?"

"I couldn't predict the actions of a crazy woman, Tom."

He leaned on the bar. "According to what Mandy told me in the ER, this woman had been bothering her for years, and you knew about it."

"I've known that Cindy has been bullying Mandy for less than two months. I wanted to talk to Cindy, but your daughter wouldn't let me. She insisted that it would only make it worse. I was respecting her wishes until last week when I overheard the conversation between the two of them. Did she tell you I was with the district administrator, showing him the video when my office assistant called me?"

"No, she left that part out," he admitted, taking another drink of the brandy.

"She wasn't thinking very clearly, I'm sure. The fact is, I had every intention of ending Cindy's employment, but like any profession, I couldn't do that without due cause, could I?"

"Instead, it took violence to end her employment," he spat.

"No, it took me overhearing her using inappropriate language to another co-worker for her to end her employment. I moved quickly and went through the proper channels. I had no way of knowing Cindy was going to go postal on Mandy. You've known both of them a hell of a lot longer than I have. Why didn't you stop the bullying?"

"I didn't know about it, or I would have!" he exclaimed. I raised one brow and looked him up, then down.

"Would you have? Or would you have used it as another lesson to help curb your daughter's wild ways?"

"You have no right to ask that, Nick," he said, slamming the glass down on the bar.

"Maybe I don't, but for the life of me, I'm trying to figure out why you brought me out here? Was it to accuse me of not taking care of your daughter in a professional situation that I had no control over? Was it to use the incident on Friday to tell me I'm not good enough for your daughter? Or was it to actually talk about how much I love her, and her children, because I sure as hell can't figure it out."

"None of the above. I brought you out here to show you something." He pushed off the bar and went to a shelf, pulling down a wooden box. He brought it back to the bar and set it in front of me. I ran my hand over the intricately carved crest of a lion with a crown.

I glanced up at him. "Scottish?"

"Yes, my grandparents came here from Scotland when they were first married. They had planned to stay only a few weeks but fell so in love with Minnesota they could never leave. The land we walk on is their homestead."

"Wow, I had no idea."

He took a key from his pocket and opened the lock on the box. "My parents passed before my grandparents did, so the property was left to the firstborn grandson, me. I've tried to be a good keeper of the land, but I've been keeping something else for as many years."

He flipped the box open and pulled out a smaller one, handing it to me. I accepted and opened the lid, surprised by the large blue topaz encircled by diamonds. "This is gorgeous, Tom. Why is it out here?"

"I brought it out here a few days ago. I've suspected you might be the one who would do the right thing and ask her father for her hand, even though she's clearly old enough to make her own decisions."

I glanced up from the ring. "Why doesn't Suzie wear this ring? It's stunning."

"My grandmother was still alive the first few years we were married. She died two weeks before Mandy was born. She never got to meet her but made me promise if we had a girl that the ring would go to her. I made that promise then, and I will keep it now."

I closed the box and set it on the bar. "She's

been married before, Tom. Why did you wait?"

He picked the box up and opened it, taking out the ring. "I waited because she hadn't found the man who would treat her the same way my grandfather treated my grandmother. Jacob wasn't the man she thought he was. If he had given her this ring, how do you think she would feel about it now?"

I eyed the gem in his hand. "I suppose she wouldn't be able to wear it. She would find it disdainful, yet feel guilty because it was her grandmother's."

"So, you see my reason for withholding it?" he asked.

"Absolutely, if I was a father, I guess I would have done the same thing."

He set it back in the box and handed it to me. "When you're ready to ask her, you have the right ring."

I reached out and accepted the box. It was more than a ring. It was a peace offering, a continuation of the family, and a passing of a torch.

I put my hand out and he shook it firmly, "Thank you, Tom. I promise to love her the way your grandfather loved your grandmother."

"You already do, Nick." He smiled, drank the rest of his brandy and turned the lights out in the workshop.

I sat in the dark and listened to his steps until I could no longer hear the crunch of the gravel. I gazed around the shop in the dim afternoon light and knew I had just found my head elf.

"Why do women go out at midnight to shop?" Ben asked as we sat in my kitchen, eating pie straight from the pan.

"I suppose it's for the same reason men go out into the woods to hunt at the crack of dawn … because they enjoy it."

He thought about that for a few minutes then nodded. "I suppose that's as good a reason as any, but what's wrong with shopping at a normal time of day. Why do they have to go and stand in line the day after Thanksgiving?"

"For the deals, my boy," I teased, using his mother's tone of voice.

"I can't believe we just ate pie at one a.m." His voice held a tinge of awe and a lot of fatigue.

"I was too full to eat all the pie I wanted at dinner this afternoon. Good thing we know the pie baker." I winked and he set his fork down.

"Liberty didn't make these pies," he said, leaning back in my kitchen chair.

"I know Adam helped, but it tastes like Liberty's pecan pie to me."

"Adam made them all by himself. Liberty was having problems and couldn't come over to help him at Grandma's, so he tied on his apron and did it himself."

I furrowed a brow. "Problems with her MS or problems at the bakery?"

"If you want my opinion, I think it was a set-up," he said and I noticed his eyes filled with mischief.

I carried the forks to the sink and ushered him into the living room. "A set-up, you say?"

He sat on the couch and tucked his feet under him. "Yup, a set-up. Adam is Liberty's apprentice at the bakery, right?" I nodded in answer. "He's been working there for two years now and he wants to take the test to become a … a …" he snapped his fingers looking for the right word.

"A journeyman baker," I answered.

He clapped. "Yes, that, but I guess he doesn't have much confidence that he can do it because he has Down Syndrome."

"I don't think he has to take the test for another year."

"I know that, but you gotta understand that Adam doesn't. He doesn't really compute time very well. He always thinks he might have to take the test tomorrow. He doesn't like tests."

"I can understand that. A lot of people don't like tests. I'm still confused as to why she would set him up."

"Maybe I should have said, helping him gain confidence? Like she wanted him to do it on his own to prove to himself he could."

"Ahh, that makes much more sense. Well, if

that pie was any indication of his skills, he's going to be just fine."

"Maybe you should tell him that the next time you see him. He really likes you, Nick."

I patted him on the shoulder. "I'll be sure to do that." I watched his fingers drumming on his leg and his tired, yet wired body. "Is something bothering you, Ben?"

He checked the clock on the mantle. "I'm worried about mom. She probably shouldn't be out shopping when it's only been a week since she got hurt. Maybe we should call her."

"She's with Grandma and Aunt December. They won't let her do more than she should. Besides, Esther is there, and she's been a real taskmaster lately."

He nodded but didn't look convinced. "I still don't like it."

"I don't like that you feel such a responsibility towards your mom at such a young age. You're supposed to be young and carefree at eleven, not worried about the adults in your life."

He shrugged. "I don't really remember what that's like, to be honest. I've always taken care of my mom and Esther. Someone had to be the man of the house. My father sure as heck wasn't."

I pulled out my phone and sent a text to Mandy. *"Ben is worried you're doing too much. Are you okay?"*

I saw the bubble pop up and waited for the text, then read it to Ben. "*We are on our way back to Snowberry. Ben was right. I shouldn't have gone shopping after the long day at Mom's. They're going to drop us off in half an hour."*

Ben chuckled at being right and I typed back quickly. *"I'll take him over there and we'll be waiting."*

"I told you," he said when I stowed the phone in my pocket.

"Let me tell you a little secret about women, Ben. Sometimes, they need to go out and try something, even if we don't think it's a good idea. They need to figure that out for themselves. Maybe, like tonight, they discover we were right and they shouldn't have tried it, but maybe, they will have the best night of their lives. Do you understand what I mean?"

"I get it, Nick. I just don't want her to get hurt worse than she already is. She's always one fall or one infection away from being hurt and there's no one here to help her. It's nice that my grandma and grandpa are helping us more now. I can tell it makes a difference in Mom's life."

I squeezed his shoulder and nodded. "Me, too. She doesn't get as stressed out now that she has someone to turn to."

"She wants to turn to you the most, though," he admitted and I raised one brow.

"You think so?"

"She told me so. I just don't think she knows she did. She was talking in her sleep one night and said she wants to spend forever with you."

I chuckled, but my heart grew in my chest. "I'm

not sure we can take sleep talking as the gospel truth, but I feel the same way. As a matter of fact, I need to ask you something."

"Shoot," he said, swinging his legs off the couch and sitting up.

"I talked to your grandpa earlier tonight and he gave me something that's pretty special."

"What was it?" he asked and I stood, taking the box off the small secretary desk in the corner. I handed it to him and his eyes concentrated on it for a long time. "I've seen this ring before. I think it was my great-grandmother's ring. I remember seeing it in pictures."

"How could you forget it, right? It's the same color blue as your mom's eyes."

He glanced up at me. "It kind of is, isn't it? What are you doing with it?"

"Your grandpa gave it to me, so I can ask your mom to marry me. First, I want to ask your permission."

He sat up straight and the box shook in his hand. "Why are you asking my permission? You're supposed to ask her father's permission."

"I did that, too, that's why he gave me the ring. The way I see it, though, you've been the man of the family for the last six years, right?" He nodded and I took the ring from his hand. "It seems to me then that you should have a say in whether I'm the kind of guy who deserves your mother's love. I need to know you believe I will take care of her, and love her, the way a man is supposed to love and take care of a woman."

He was vibrating as he sat on the couch and then in one move, he had his arms wrapped around my neck and his head over my shoulder. "I've been praying for this day."

I rubbed his back and smiled since he couldn't see me. "Does that mean I have your permission to marry your mom?"

His chin bobbed against my shoulder then he sat back down on the couch. "When are you going to ask her?"

I stowed the ring box in the safe on the bookshelf then turned back to him. "I have an idea, but if I'm going to pull it off, I'm going to need your help."

He grabbed his coat and shoved his arms in the sleeves. "You can count on me, Nick. Just don't tell Esther, she can't keep a secret to save her soul."

I slung my arm over his shoulder and laughed as we walked to his house. "We'll keep this between you, me, and your grandpa. We're meeting Sunday privately after dinner. He's my head elf. You can be my right-hand man. We have some plans to make, and together, we'll make this a Christmas she will never forget."

Chapter Twenty-Four

"Are you all ready, Santa?"

I turned toward the soft voice behind me, and Mandy was walking toward me, dressed in the sweetest Mrs. Claus dress I had ever seen.

I pulled her into my arms. "Why, Mrs. Claus, aren't you beautiful this morning."

She laughed softly and tugged on my beard a little. "I've worn this dress every year for the last five years you've been part of Coats for Kids."

"I know, and I've gone home and been in pain thinking about you in that dress for the last five years. Tonight, I'm not going to be in pain, though. Tonight, I'm going to be in you."

She swatted my shoulder and looked around a little. "Santa, who's the naughty one now? You're going to have to put your own name on the list."

"Trust me when I say it's already on there, multiple times." I started laughing, "Ho, ho, ho, Santa's getting coal."

She rested her head on my big fat chest and laughed hysterically, trying to remain quiet as the kids were gathering in front of the curtains for the arrival of Santa.

"I love you, Mr. Klaus," she whispered, raising her head for a kiss.

I gave her one through my scratchy fake beard. "That will have to do, for now, Mrs. Claus, but as soon as we're alone, the beard goes, and so does the dress."

"The kids are home tonight, Nick," she said, patting my chest, and I lightly grasped her braced wrist.

"Not until four, though. Your mom and dad are taking them Christmas shopping, remember?"

She stepped back and straightened my suit, fixing the beard to make sure it hung correctly. "That's true, but only because we will be cleaning up the community center from the event this afternoon."

I picked up her hand and inspected the brace. "Too bad your arm is going to be sore after you've played Christmas carols all morning. Santa will have to take you home and give you a massage instead of cleaning up cookies and spilled hot chocolate."

She snickered and rolled her eyes. "Santa is a bad, bad boy. I like it."

I kissed her again chastely on the cheek and picked up my heavy red bag of toys. "Then let's get this done, so you can sit on Santa's lap and tell him exactly what you want for Christmas."

She raised one brow, looked me up and down and then, without a word, snuck between the curtains. In seconds, I heard Jingle Bells on the piano and the kids started singing boisterously. I cleared my throat a couple of times and said a few words in my thick German accent. I knew all these kids, so to keep them guessing, I always revert to my childhood accent when I put on the beard.

The song finished and I slipped my white-gloved hand through the crack in the curtains, ready to pull it back quickly. It was a tradition and I waited for the first kid to spot it.

"Santa! Santa is here!" I heard a voice and then Mandy started playing the chorus of Jingle Bells again, just on the high keys.

"Santa is here?" she asked, and the kids all yelled, "Yes!"

I could see them pointing in my mind, even though I couldn't actually see them. I pushed my hand all the way through the curtains and waved it a couple times to get the kids' attention, then pulled it back in.

"I don't see Santa," Mandy said from the piano and the kids all started talking at once. "Maybe we should call Santa and see if he's really here?" she asked the kids. Again, a huge *Yes!* roared through the center.

The music stopped and then I heard my cue. "Santa, are you here?"

I pulled the curtain aside and walked out onto the floor of the center. "Ho, ho, ho! Merry Christmas!" I chortled and dropped the bag to brace myself.

The kids crowded around me, hugging any

open space they could find on my suit. I patted heads and winked at the woman trying to control them all.

I watched the line of kids waiting to sit on my lap dwindle down to the last one. After hearing the wishes of over thirty kids, I was beginning to get nervous for the final one. Esther waited patiently, the last in line, while her friend Amanda told me about the doll she wanted for Christmas.

"That sounds like a very nice doll, Amanda. Santa will see what his elves can do," I promised, taking a candy cane from the basket and handing it to her. "You have a Merry Christmas, sweetheart."

Amanda jumped down off my lap and skipped over to the table where Suzie had cookies and hot chocolate waiting. I motioned to Esther to come over and she glanced toward her mom, who smiled at her and nodded. I helped my sweet little girl onto my lap and tried not to give myself away.

"Merry Christmas, Esther," I said in my fake voice.

"Merry Christmas, Santa. How do you know my name?"

I ho-ho'd and tried to make my fake belly jiggle. "I've known you since you were a wee one, Esther.

Let's see, last year, I brought you a white horse with sparkly hair, right?"

She nodded. "That was exactly what I wanted. Thank you, Santa!"

I squeezed the little girl's shoulders. "You're very welcome. Have you been a good girl this year, Esther?"

She folded her hands and shrugged. "I think so. I talked back to my mom a few times and wasn't very nice to a boy in my class once, but he was asking for it."

"I don't suppose his name was Xander?" I asked, very seriously.

Her eyes got round like saucers and she nodded. "That's him, but don't be mad at him, Santa. I thought he didn't like me, but it turns out he was just sad because someone was picking on him. I've forgiven him and we're friends now."

"Well, that's good to hear, little Esther. I should take him off the naughty list then?"

She clasped her hands together tightly. "Please do, Santa. He's not bad. He was just sad."

I patted her back. "I'll make sure my elves bring him something nice. What can I bring for you this year? I know for sure you're on the nice list. You are always kind to your friends and you've helped your mom a lot this year when she's been hurt."

She eyed me suspiciously and I swallowed, afraid she made me. "How did you know my mom got hurt?"

I chortled again. "Santa knows everything, Esther. Remember the whole *he sees you when you're sleeping, he knows when you're awake* thing?"

She nodded. "That's kind of creepy, though, Santa."

I laughed in my natural voice and covered it with a cough. "It is sort of creepy, but I don't actually watch you sleep. My elves keep watch every so often to see if you're behaving the way a good girl should. They reported to me that you've been exceptionally good. I was sorry to hear about your broken arm, though."

She pulled up her sleeve a little. "Thanks, Santa. My arm is healed now. Look, you can barely see the scar." She pointed at the thin line and I lowered my fake spectacles to get a good look at it.

"My, you're right. Someone did a good job with that. I'm glad it healed so well. So, do you want a new horse again this Christmas? I know you have a nice collection."

She looked nervous but shook her head. "Not this year, Santa. I was going to ask for something for my mom."

I patted her back a couple of times. "You can ask for something for your mom, but I'll still bring you something, too."

"I was going to ask that you bring my mom Nick for Christmas, but not just for Christmas morning, but like for good. I mean for, like, ever."

My insides froze for a moment and then melted into all kinds of gooey chocolate. "Hmm, what makes you think your mom wants this Nick for, like, ever?"

She sat up taller and clasped her tiny hands over mine. "I know Mom loves Nick."

"This Nick, he sounds pretty special." I tried not to choke on the words when I forced them out. There was nothing like talking about yourself, when you're pretending to be someone else, to make you feel like a fish out of water.

"I'm talking about Nick S. Klaus. He's the principal at my school, and our next-door neighbor. He's been in love with my mom for lots of years and I know she's in love with him, too. I want us all to be a family, so he can live at our house instead of going to his every night."

"I see, I see," I said, buying time. "That's a fair thing to ask for. Have you talked to your mom and Nick about it?"

She leaned in, and her breath tickled my ear. "I just did. I love you, Nick."

Then she climbed down off my lap, calmly walked to the table, and helped herself to a cookie.

Chapter Twenty-Five

"Are you nervous, Nick?" Ben asked as I stood by the gymnasium door in the dark. The elementary kids were almost done with their concert and it was nearly time for my solo.

"I think I'm going to throw up," I said, my voice shaking. "Maybe this isn't a good idea. Maybe I should do it later."

Ben leveled a look at me that said *too late to back out now*. He handed me the Santa hat from his back pocket and I put it on. "Just pretend everyone is in their underwear. That's what mom tells us to do."

I covered my mouth to keep my laughter from being heard over the kids. "That's sort of gross."

"I know, right? But it works. You don't have time to be nervous when you're grossed out."

I shook out my shoulders and nodded. "Good point. Okay, here comes the last song."

He snuck back in the door to sit next to his grandparents and I waited while the kids sang the first verse of Jingle Bells. By the time I got out onto the floor, the kids were finishing the final verse. Mandy played an energetic jingle bell finish and the audience burst into applause.

I took the microphone and tapped it a couple times until I had everyone's attention. The room quieted and I brought the mic to my mouth, my hand shaking as I looked at all the people, but only saw one woman.

"Thank you all for coming tonight to the annual elementary holiday sing. For those who don't know me, I'm Principal Nick S. Klaus. I have a little surprise for Ms. Alexander this evening. The kids and I were talking one day, while she was making copies about how she never gets to enjoy the concerts because she always has to do all the work." I frowned and the audience laughed as the kids all gave a thumbs down. "So, I thought tonight, if you would so indulge us, the kids and I would perform a song for her. That is if everyone can wait for those milk and cookies that were tempting me out in the hallway."

Ben carried a chair onto the floor for his mom and she looked to me and then him a couple of times. I winked and she gave me *what the heck* hands but sat on the chair.

"When I was growing up in Germany, my mom always made sure we listened to plenty of American Christmas carols. Our favorite was *Up on the Housetop*." There was a ripple of laughter through the audience when they got the joke. I walked over to Mandy and took her hand. "Tonight, I give you *Up on the Housetop*, Nick S. Klaus style."

The lights went down in the gymnasium and

the kids started clapping as Ben led them in a pop version of the old carol. "Down through the chimney with *gut heilig* Nick," they sang while Mandy laughed hysterically. She gazed up at me and all I saw was the love in her eyes. We both turned back to the kids as Ben led them through the final verse, but instead of singing the same ending line, they all shouted, "Will you marry Principal Klaus?"

The audience began clapping wildly as I dropped to one knee and pulled the ring out of my pocket. I held it out to her. "Mandy, I've waited for five lonely Christmases to ask you this, and I don't want to wait through another. Will you be my wife and make this the first Christmas of our forever?"

She stared at the ring and her hands came to her mouth. "Is that my Grandmother's ring?"

I nodded. "Your Dad gave it to me. Said he had been saving it until the day the right man asked him for permission to marry his daughter. I guess he thought that was me."

"Mom!" Esther hissed from the group of kids edging toward us. "Say yes!"

The audience burst into laughter and Mandy used the moment of distraction to her advantage. "I would love to be Mrs. Klaus forever."

I slipped the ring on her finger and she threw her arms around my neck. I stood with her and all the kids gathered around, hugging us and clapping. She kissed my lips and they all pretended to gag, but the whole gymnasium was filled with laughter and happiness.

"How did you pull this off, Nick?" she asked when I set her on her feet.

I picked Esther up in my arms and Ben hugged his mom.

"His name isn't Nick Santa Klaus for nothing, Mom." Ben winked and Mandy glanced up at me, surprised. I blew her a kiss, and in the twinkle of her eye, I saw all my dreams come true.

"Wake up, Mrs. Almost Klaus," I whispered, kissing her awake.

She rubbed at her eyes. "Nick, the kids are still asleep. We don't have to get up yet."

"I know we don't, but before this busy day begins, I want to give you your present."

She sat up slowly and stretched, her nightshirt falling dangerously low, but I forced my thoughts away from her sweet body. It had been four days since the proposal at school and they hadn't gone home except to get clothes. They were moving in, with me, and selling the house next door. It would be a clean start for our family, and I planned to make a lasting memory this morning.

I climbed off the bed and helped her sit up, grateful that her wrist no longer sported the black brace, and the bruise on her side was gone. She bent over and put her legs on, then stood and joined me at the door.

"Go start the fireplace while I use the bathroom," she whispered and I nodded, leaving her at the bathroom and heading to the living room. Our freshly decorated tree waited with all the gifts underneath, but I stopped short when I saw two gifts I hadn't put there. They were snuggled in sleeping bags next to each other and they both bolted upright when they heard me.

"Merry Christmas, Nick!" they both whispered.

I sat on the floor, hugging them both. "Merry Christmas to both of you. I wasn't expecting to see you out here."

Ben stood and turned on the fireplace then came back to where we sat. "The last few days haven't seemed real. We thought if we slept under the tree, and were still here Christmas morning, then it wasn't a dream."

I hugged him and ruffled his hair. "It's not a dream, Ben. Here we are on Christmas morning and we're all together. Honestly, it felt a little like a dream when I woke up next to your mom this morning, so I understand."

Esther checked down the hallway. "Where is Mom? Is she still sleeping?"

"I'm right here," she said, joining us by the tree. "I guess you were up after all."

I pointed to the sleeping bags. "They slept under the tree."

"Santa Claus came!" Esther cried out when she saw the packages under the tree. "I mean the other

Santa Claus!"

We all burst into giggles and I held my finger up. "Before we open all those pretty packages, I have a special gift for you three."

I handed Ben an envelope and he opened it, while Mandy and Esther looked over his shoulder. Ben glanced up at me. "I don't understand what this is."

Mandy took it from his hands and reread it. "This is a letter from our lawyer to the family judge, Ben." She looked up at me then back to her two kids, "Nick, the court won't let Jacob sign away his rights."

"I know, but you said if there was a step-parent waiting in the wings to adopt them, the court would reconsider it. Kate drew up that letter to tell the judge there is someone waiting to adopt Ben and Esther. I want to be their dad, and I will support them emotionally and financially. The letter is just a rough draft. If you, and the kids, agree to let me adopt them, then we can finish the letter and send it to the judge."

Ben and Esther almost knocked me over when they barreled into me. "Yes, we want you to adopt us, Nick!"

"Can I call you Daddy?" Esther asked, and I patted her face.

"First, your mom and I have to get married, sweetheart," I reminded her, and she nodded.

"Okay, but then can I?"

Mandy laughed happily and pulled her daughter onto her lap. "As far as I'm concerned, you can call him that now, Esther."

Esther jumped up off her mom's lap and gave a rather dainty fist pump. "I've always wanted a daddy!"

Mandy held the letter to her chest and her chin trembled. "Thank you, Nick. I didn't expect this. You're full of surprises."

"I have one more," I said, handing her an empty photo album.

"What's this?"

"Before I can adopt the kids, we have to get married. That's an empty photo album I want to fill with pictures of our wedding day."

She flipped it open and there were four tickets to San Francisco in the front. She raised one eyebrow. "Honeymoon?"

"I was hoping," I winked and she checked the dates on the ticket. "That's spring break."

"It is. My sisters will be together there then, and I want them to meet you and the kids."

"That doesn't give us much time to plan a wedding," she said, frowning and I took her hand.

"I know, and you can take all the time you want to plan the wedding. I know you didn't have the wedding of your dreams the first time and I want to give you that. If we aren't married by the time April rolls around, we will just call it a spring break getaway."

She looked at the tickets and then to the kids. "I've been thinking over the last few days about what kind of ceremony I want. I think a small wedding on the farm with my family and our friends from work would be perfect. You know I'm not marrying you for the wedding."

I leaned over and kissed her soft lips. "No, you're marrying me for what comes after."

The kids groaned and gagged until we broke apart laughing. "Okay, enough sappy stuff. We can talk to your mom and dad about it later today. For now, who wants to open presents?" I asked and Esther jumped around excitedly.

"Let's give Nick his present!" she said, still bouncing like a jumping bean.

Mandy touched the tip of Esther's nose and smiled. "Good plan. Be a good little elf and help your brother bring it over."

They carried a large, oddly shaped package over and laid it on my lap. "I have no idea what this could be."

"Less talk, more unwrapping." Mandy motioned and I saluted her then tore off the paper. I saw my name scrawled across the top of the black case.

"You didn't," I said, pulling the paper the rest of the way off the package. "This is my old Schrammel guitar."

"All the way from Germany," Ben said very seriously.

I opened the case and took out the beautiful instrument, strumming the strings in disbelief. "I can't believe I'm holding this right now. How did you do it?"

Mandy smiled, and laying a finger aside of her nose, she winked. "They don't call me almost Mrs. Klaus for nothing."

The Snowberry Series

Snow Daze

Trapped in an elevator with a handsome stranger was the perfect meet-cute, but Dr. Snow Daze wasn't interested in being the heroine of any romance novel. A serious researcher at Providence Hospital in Snowberry, Minnesota, Snow doesn't have time for a personal life, which was exactly the way she liked it.

Dully Alexander hated elevators, until he was stuck in one with a beautiful snow angel. Intrigued by her gorgeous white hair, and her figure-hugging wheelchair, he knows he'll do anything to be her hero.

When a good old-fashioned Minnesota blizzard traps them at her apartment, he takes advantage of the crackling fire, whispered secrets on the couch, and stolen kisses in the night. Dully will stop at nothing to convince Snow she deserves her own happily ever after.

December Kiss

It's nearly Christmas in Snowberry Minnesota, but Jay Alexander is feeling anything but jolly. Stuck in the middle of town square with a flat tire on his worn-out wheelchair leaves him feeling grinchy.

December Kiss has only been in Snowberry for a few months when she happens upon this broken-down boy next door. His sandy brown hair and quirky smile has her hoisting his wheelchair into the back of her four horse Cherokee.

When a December romance blooms, Jay wants to give December just one thing for Christmas, her brother. Will Jay get his December Kiss under the mistletoe Christmas Eve?

Noel's Hart

Noel Kiss is a successful businessman, but adrift in his personal life. After he reconnects with his twin sister, Noel realizes he's bored, lonely, and searching for a change. That change might be waiting for him in Snowberry, Minnesota.

Savannah Hart is known in Snowberry as 'the smile maker' in Snowberry, Minnesota. She has poured blood, sweat, and tears into her flower emporium and loves spreading cheer throughout the community. She uses those colorful petals to hide her secrets from the people of Snowberry, but there's one man who can see right through them.

On December twenty-fourth, life changes for both Noel and Savannah. He finds a reason for change, and she finds the answer to a prayer. Desperate for relief, Savannah accepts Noel's crazy proposal, telling herself it will be easy to say goodbye when the time comes, but she's fooling no one.

Noel has until Valentine's Day to convince Savannah his arms are the shelter she's been yearning for. If he can't, the only thing he'll be holding on February 14th is a broken heart.

April Melody

April Melody loved her job as bookkeeper and hostess of Kiss's Café in Snowberry, Minnesota. What she didn't love was having to hide who she was on the inside, because of what people saw on the outside. April may not be able to hear them, but she could read the lies on their lips.

Martin Crow owns Crow's Hair and Nails, an upscale salon in the middle of bustling Snowberry. Crow hid from the world in the tiny town, and focused on helping women find their inner goddess. What he wasn't expecting to find was one of Snowberry's goddesses standing outside his apartment door.

Drawn together by their love of music, April and Crow discover guilt and hatred will steal their future. Together they learn to let love and forgiveness be the melody and harmony in their hearts.

Liberty Belle

Main Street is bustling in Snowberry, Minnesota, and nobody knows that better than the owner of the iconic bakery, the Liberty Belle. Handed the key to her namesake at barely twenty-one, Liberty has worked day and night to keep her parents' legacy alive. Now, three years later, she's a hotter mess than the batch of pies baking in her industrial-sized oven.

Photographer Bram Alexander has had his viewfinder focused on the heart of one woman since returning to Snowberry. For the last three years she's kept him at arm's length, but all bets are off when he finds her injured and alone on the bakery floor.

Liberty found falling in love with Bram easy, but convincing her tattered heart to trust him was much harder. Armed with small town determination and a heart of gold, Bram shows Liberty frame-by-frame how learning to trust him is as easy as pie.

Wicked Winifred

Winifred Papadopoulos, Freddie to her few friends, has a reputation in Snowberry, Minnesota. Behind her back, and occasionally to her face, she's known as Wicked Winifred. Freddie uses her sharp tongue as a defense mechanism to keep people at bay. The truth is, her heart was broken beyond repair at sixteen, and she doesn't intend to get close to anyone ever again. She didn't foresee a two-minute conversation at speed dating as the catalyst to turn her life upside down.

Flynn Steele didn't like dating. He liked speed dating even less. When his business partner insisted, he reluctantly agreed, sure it would be a waste of time, until he met the Wicked Witch of the West. He might not like dating, but the woman behind the green makeup intrigued him.

A downed power pole sets off a series of events neither Flynn nor Winifred saw coming. Their masks off, and their hearts open, they have until Halloween to decide if the scars of the past will bring them together or tear them apart. Grab your broomstick and hang on tight. This is going to be a bumpy ride…

Nick S. Klaus

Nick S. Klaus is a patient man, but living next door to Mandy Alexander for five years has him running low this Christmas season. He wants nothing more than to make her his Mrs. Klaus, but she'd rather pretend he isn't real.

Mandy Alexander is a single mom and full-time teacher. She doesn't have time to date or for the entanglements it can cause. Even if she did have time, getting involved with her next-door neighbor, and co-worker, Nick S. Klaus, had disaster written all over it.

This Christmas, Nick's determined to teach Mandy that love doesn't have to be complicated, and he's got two of the cutest Christmas elves to help him get the job done. Will this be the year Santa finally gets his Mrs. Klaus under the mistletoe?

About The Author

Katie Mettner

Katie Mettner writes small-town romantic tales filled with epic love stories and happily-ever-afters. She proudly wears the title of, 'the only person to lose her leg after falling down the bunny hill,' and loves decorating her prosthetic leg with the latest fashion trends. She lives in Northern Wisconsin with her own happily-ever-after and three mini-mes. Katie has a massive addiction to coffee and Twitter, and a lessening aversion to Pinterest — now that she's quit trying to make the things she pins.

A Note To My Readers

People with disabilities are just that—people. We are not 'differently abled' because of our disability. We all have different abilities and interests, and the fact that we may or may not have a physical or intellectual disability doesn't change that. The disabled community may have different needs, but we are productive members of society who also happen to be husbands, wives, moms, dads, sons, daughters, sisters, brothers, friends, and co-workers. People with disabilities are often disrespected and portrayed two different ways; as helpless or as heroically inspirational for doing simple, basic activities.

As a disabled author who writes disabled characters, my focus is to help people without disabilities understand the real-life disability issues we face like discrimination, limited accessibility, housing, employment opportunities, and lack of people first language. I want to change the way others see our community by writing strong characters who go after their dreams, and find their true love, without shying away from what it is like to be a person with a disability. Another way I can educate people without disabilities is to help them understand our terminology. We, as the disabled community, have worked to establish what we call People First Language. This isn't a case of being politically correct. Rather, it is a way to acknowledge and communicate with a person with a disability in a respectful way by eliminating generalizations, assumptions, and stereotypes.

As a person with disabilities, I appreciate when readers take the time to ask me what my preferred language is. Since so many have asked, I thought I would include a small sample of the people-first language we use in the disabled community. This language also applies when leaving reviews and talking about books that feature characters with disabilities. The most important thing to remember when you're talking to people with disabilities is that we are people first! If you ask us what our preferred terminology is regarding our disability, we will not only tell you, but be glad you asked! If you would like more information about people first language, you will find a disability resource guide on my website.

Instead of: He is handicapped.
Use: He is a person with a disability.

Instead of: She is differently abled.
Use: She is a person with a disability.

Instead of: He is mentally retarded.
Use: He has a developmental or intellectual disability.

Instead of: She is wheelchair-bound.
Use: She uses a wheelchair.

Instead of: He is a cripple.
Use: He has a physical disability.

Instead of: She is a midget or dwarf.
Use: She is a person of short stature or a little person.

Instead of: He is deaf and mute.
Use: He is deaf or he has a hearing disability.

Instead of: She is a normal or healthy person.
Use: She is a person without a disability.

Instead of: That is handicapped parking.
Use: That is accessible parking.

Instead of: He has overcome his disability.
Use: He is successful and productive.

Instead of: She is suffering from vision loss.
Use: She is a person who is blind or visually disabled.

Instead of: He is brain damaged.
Use: He is a person with a traumatic brain injury.

Other Books by Katie Mettner

The Fluffy Cupcake Series (2)

The Kontakt Series (2)

The Sugar Series (5)

The Northern Lights Series (4)

The Snowberry Series (7)

The Kupid's Cove Series (4)

The Magnificent Series (2)

The Bells Pass Series (5)

The Dalton Sibling Series (3)

The Raven Ranch Series (2)

The Butterfly Junction Series (2)

A Christmas at Gingerbread Falls

Someone in the Water (Paranormal)

White Sheets & Rosy Cheeks (Paranormal)

The Secrets Between Us

After Summer Ends (Lesbian Romance)

Finding Susan (Lesbian Romance)

Torched

Printed in Great Britain
by Amazon